STATIC DREAMS

VOLUME TWO

A Dark Anthology from Twisted Minds

STATIC DREAMS

VOLUME TWO

An Dark Anthology from Twisted Minds

edited by tara caribou

Raw Earth Ink
2019

This book is a work of fiction.

Copyright 2019 by tara caribou

All rights reserved. No part of this book may be reproduced or used in any manner without express written permission from the author except in the case of quotations used in a book review in which a clear link to the source of the quote and its author is required.

First paperback edition December 2019

Book and cover design by tara caribou

ISBN 978-1-7330808-3-5 (paperback)

Published by Raw Earth Ink
PO Box 39332
Ninilchik, Alaska USA 99639
www.taracaribou.com

Table of Contents

Introduction 3
That Ol' Devil's Work *by* Patrick Walts 5
Daniel & the Gryphon *by* Christopher Allen Waldrop 29
The Seaside Lolly Shop *by* Mark Towse 41
To the Beginning *by* River Dixon & tara caribou 77
The Cat *by* Mark Ryan 109
The Truth Lies in Darkness *by* Bobby Blade 127
Grimm *by* M. Ennenbach 149
Reverberation *by* Sam Kirk 197
The Guest House *by* Chris Nelson 227
Author Biographies 263

Introduction

    Night has long since fallen and the shadows which surround you, invading your mind without asking, they beckon you to open your eyes wider.

    You are unable to look away from the giant screen before you. The dark images command your attention, your feet are unable to move and yet you now find yourself somehow sitting on an overstuffed, somewhat worn chair, remote still in hand. The room around you lit only by the gruesome and agonizing images moving across the flickering screen. The shadows stir behind you even as the memories of your previous dreams have long faded and the nightmares of those before you rise in the garish glow.

    Your thumb hesitates before clicking the center button of the mysterious remote again. A young girl lies on a hospital bed, her arms tethered as she screams the name of her brother over and over, her head and extremities covered in multi-colored wires, while men in stark lab coats jot notes on their clipboards. You push the button. A boy cries in the corner of a dark room, a ratty teddy bear absorbing his tears with blank eyes, watching the snoring husk of his father on the lazy-boy, the smell of beer and haunting memories clouding his dreams. You push the button. A woman, heavily pregnant, weeps upon her bed, as the terms of her grim contract come due before her eyes, stacks of books covering the mattress and floor; every dream she could have hoped for has come true, and now it's become her worst nightmare. Though you try, you cannot look away and you push the button once more...

THAT OL' DEVIL'S WORK

by Patrick Walts

I never asked Pa why we fed the fields. It was just what we'd always done, as far back as I could remember. "Cotton won't grow without it," was all he'd tell us, my sister and I, and our father wasn't the sort of father who was open to questions and discussion. In other words, we did as we were told.

As the oldest, I was the first to be taken aside and given a full explanation when Pa felt I was ready to receive it.

He brought me out back behind the barn, over the collapsing, weed-entangled chicken wire fence surrounding it, and through the labyrinth of rusty old tractor parts that'd littered the yard since long before I was born.

I'd seen the sweatbox from the outside, but until that day, Pa hadn't felt I was ready to go in and see the uglier side of what we were charged with doing once a month. Before he opened the door, he told me the whole story, from start to finish, and I don't think I so much as blinked the entire time he spoke.

"I got this farm cheap because folks 'round here all thought it was cursed. Warned me not to buy it. Even the bank. Well, I thought that was hogwash, and I signed those papers. Signed my soul away, too, but I didn't find that out until later on, of course.

"Y'see, son, the land's got a taste for blood. Started with the Indians, but that's a story for another time.

"Way back before the war of Northern aggression, this ol' boy by the name of Arthur Baggarley, who owned this land, well, he had a whole slew of slaves workin' for him on it. Used to whip 'em 'til they was half dead anytime they got outta line, or even just 'cause he felt like it. Talk was that he consorted with some of the females, but most reckoned that was all Yankee gossip. Wicked, wicked man, though. Heck, I wouldn't put it pass 'im.

"They bled a lot, them people. They bled, they sweat, and they shed tears, and the soil soaked it all up, took a liking to it. In return, the land gave ol' Baggarley the biggest cotton crop in North Carolina.

"Well, one night they decided amongst theirselves that they wasn't gonna take that kinda treatment no more. And, 'course, you can hardly blame 'em. You wouldn't do a dog the way he done them folk. Yessir, dang shame how they got treated back in them days. But that was the 1860s and this is the 1960s. Folks know better now.

"Anyhow, they busted down the front door and run wild throughout the whole house, smashed everything to bits 'fore ol' Baggarley come down the stairs in his sleepin' gown with a lantern in his hand.

"They tore that man limb from limb, and killed his wife, too. Some say they had their way with her, but I don't b'lieve that. They was just some fed up folks that wanted to be free. Burnt the place to the ground when that lamp hit the floor and the burnin' oil took off upside them fancy type curtains rich folks have.

"After that, they all run off, scattered all over creation. Most of 'em got snatched up and hanged, but a whole lot've 'em got away and was never heard from 'til after the war. One of 'em even wrote a book. Talked about how he wasn't 'posed to learn how to read but he went ahead and did anyhow.

"Now you think of that, boy, next time your schoolteacher tells me you ain't payin' attention in school. Some people wanna learn so bad they'll risk dyin' for it.

"Anyhow, by the time the new owners of the land came around, there wasn't no more slaves, the law'd done away with it, y'see. Couldn't nobody get nothin' to grow on this land. Not even weeds. He was gonna sell it, but one day he up and disappeared. Same thing happened to the next one. And the next one. And the next one.

"Finally, this one ol' feller sheers his toes clean off with a combine, right over there, just twenty feet away from where we're standin' right now.

"Ol' boy was smart enough to put the wound up against the hot engine and seal it up 'fore he bled to death, but he still spilt plenty of blood, sweat and tears onta that there dry, cracked ground in the meantime.

"Well, the very next day, the biggest, thickest cotton stem you ever did see sprouted up right there on that very spot.

"Now, like I said, this was a smart ol' boy, smarter'n the rest of 'em come before him, anyhow. He figured it out right quick. Spilt his blood all over the place tryin' to make it happen again. Couldn't do it.

"Even the biggest, toughest, meanest man on God's green Earth cries once in a while, though. So long as nobody sees him. And that's just *what he did, out there in the hot North Carolina sun, sweat stingin' the cuts all up and down his arm. He'd been plannin' on gettin' married to this real pretty young gal, y'see, and now he was gonna be a penniless, no account young fool with a field fulla dirt that wouldn't grow nothin'. He went to bed that night thinkin' 'bout putting his mouth on the business end of a shotgun.*

"Next mornin', though, more cotton sprung up, and on that very spot where he done broke down.

"Tears. That's what did it. Tears. He cried when he lost that toe.

"Well, after awhile of savin' up tears and blood and sweat in some waterin' cans, he sprinkled that stuff all over the dirt, and danged if that dead soil didn't come right back to life. He couldn't make enough of it on his own, though, so he started bringin' home people from town, drifters and whores and whatnot, puttin' 'em in a box in the sun and lettin' 'em get so hot they liked to die. Then he'd give 'em some water and keep on collectin' the sweat and the tears in a oil pain underneath of it. Drilled holes to let it out. If they didn't cry, he'd open up that box and beat the tar out of 'em; just wail on 'em with a switch until the tears came.

"When they finally departed this world, he'd cut 'em open at the wrists and let the blood drain out. Then he'd spread that mixture all up and down his fields.

"All that cotton made him a rich man 'fore too long, but it all came crashin' down on him when he took ill and couldn't feed the fields no more. Then he disappeared, like all the rest.

"So y'see, son, that's why we feed the fields. If we don't, we're gonna disappear, too."

Pa opened the door.

I stood there in silence for a long time and looked at the naked, portly, sweat-drenched man strapped to the workbench inside of the sweatbox. His eyes were closed, and he was mumbling something. I didn't know what he'd done for my father to have chosen him, but Pa only snatched up bad people, so I didn't feel too sorry for him.

"He's about done," said Pa, poking at the man's hairy, glistening belly with a thick, calloused working man's finger. "I think we got about all we're gonna squeeze outta this one 'fore he kicks the bucket."

I nodded. I knew what that meant. I'd never seen anyone die before, but I knew that was about to change.

Time to become a man, son.

Less than a year after that night, both Ma and Pa were killed in a car accident, and for a period of several months, I was charged with looking after my younger sister Rachel.

We carried out the ritual as we'd been taught, with me taking over father's harvesting role. I didn't care for that part too much at all, but it had to be done. I'd crack a tire iron over their hands and drag 'em to the truck. Wasn't no big deal for a boy my size.

We did just fine on our own; had no need for supervision. The law felt otherwise, though, and that's where Uncle Martin came in.

Martin was my dad's ne'er-do-well brother, his only living kin, and we'd never had much to do with him.

He'd been in and out of jail all his life, and he was a drunk. A judge saw fit to appoint him our legal guardian, though, and within weeks he'd moved into the house and started going about the business of wrecking our lives.

I tried to tell him about the fields, about the ritual, but he didn't understand what I was talking about and wouldn't let me go out at night to harvest. I told him the fields would dry up and die if they didn't get fed, but he thought I was pulling his leg and he let me know, with his hand across my face, that he wasn't going to put up with any of that nonsense.

"That's that ol' devil's work you're talkin' about, shit-for-brains. Witchcraft. You know they used to burn people alive for doin' things like that? Wasn't even *real*. Why don't you run into town and get me some whiskey?"

I bought a lot of whiskey for Uncle Martin from Henson's market. Old man Henson wouldn't sell it to me at first, but he figured out pretty quick after seeing me come in with black eyes and bruises that if I went home empty-handed, I got beat. So he stopped asking questions.

Can you imagine that? Folks back then didn't get involved in other folks' domestic affairs. He never called the police or asked if I was alright, just put the bottles in my bag week after week and took my crumpled dollar bills, never looking me in the eye.

Uncle Martin drank from sunup to sundown and didn't do much of anything else. The more he drank, the meaner he got, and he was especially upset about the land drying up and refusing to yield any cotton. He'd planned on having us pick it, doing all the work while he sat on the couch watching television and drowning in cheap liquor. He thought he'd inherited a cash cow, but all he'd gotten was a dusty ol' piece of beef jerky.

"Alright, you lil' sons a bitches!" he roared one day when he stormed into my bedroom where Rachel and I were playing checkers on the floor.

"Explain to me how y'all had the finest cotton crop for *miles* around b'fore I come in the picture, and now there ain't shit but *this*?"

He hurled a handful of dirt at us. I winced and pinched my eyes shut, then shrugged as if to show him I wasn't scared of him, even though I was. "You won't let us do the ritual."

Martin went wild. He picked up a lamp, jerking the cord out of the wall, and threw it at me. I dodged it, and the bulb shattered against the wall.

"I'm *tired* of hearing about that junk! Now what'd y'all do? Put salt down to kill the soil? You *stupid* pieces a *shit!*"

"I hate you!" screamed Rachel, tears pouring down her cheeks. "Why don't you just leave us alone? It was so much better before you came! I *hate* you!"

She took off up the stairs, and he started after her, but I rose to my feet and stood in his way.

"You leave her *alone*, y'hear?" I looked him dead in the eye.

"Alright," he said. "Okay. Have it your way, hoss. But if I find out y'all done messed up my property, I will *skin your ass alive*, understand?"

His breath smelled of liquor. I said nothing, just continued to stare.

He blinked and rubbed his eyes and staggered off into the kitchen, cussing and mumbling gibberish under his breath.

I knew at that moment that he wasn't just going to be a nuisance; he was going to be *dangerous*. He had to go.

Later that night, while lying in bed, staring at the ceiling and thinking about killing my uncle, I heard the fields growling through my open window.

"*Soon*," I whispered.

It was two weeks later when I heard a scream coming from Uncle Martin's downstairs bedroom in the middle of the night.

I leapt out of bed and rushed down to investigate, and Martin collided with me in the dark hallway. He grabbed my shoulders. "The *devil!*" he said. "I seen the devil in the window!"

I stepped back, jerking my shoulders loose of his grip.

"That wasn't no devil," I told him. "That was the fields. It wants a sacrifice. It wants you."

"I don't give a tinker's damn *what* it wants," said Martin. "How the hell you know, anyhow?"

"I told it you're the one keeping us from feeding it."

He beat me up pretty bad, but I managed to get a few good licks in, too. After convincing himself that he must've been seeing things on account of the whiskey, he went back to bed and I turned around to return to mine, wishing the fields would just hurry up and take him.

Rachel was standing behind me. She'd watched the whole thing.

"He's a mean man."

I nodded, and a drop of blood from my nose ran down my neck and disappeared under my shirt. "Sure is."

Uncle Martin saw the devil every night from there on out, and either due to drink, lack of sleep or a combination of both, he eventually got it in his head that we were behind it all.

"Tryin' to drive me crazy, aren't ya? Run me off. Well lemme tell you shit-stains somethin'. It ain't gonna work. Ya hear me? Your daddy shoulda pulled out! You're shit! *Shit!*"

He'd stomp around and break things, tussle with me a little bit, and then he'd go collapse on the couch with the television on. He'd sleep there all night sometimes, with the test pattern on the screen, oblivious to that loud, droning whine that that accompanied it.

I tried turning the television off once, but he woke up fit to be tied, said to leave it on, that it scared off the devil. I just let him be and stuffed my ears with cotton to drown out the sound. Rachel didn't care. Sound didn't bother her none.

It bothered me, though, bothered me a whole lot. Everything about Uncle Martin did.

I couldn't do away with him, though. Couldn't kill kin. That was one of Pa's rules, and obey it I would, no matter what.

Something happened one sunny afternoon, though, that shifted my outlook on the matter. He hit Rachel.

I came home from the grocery store and found Rachel parked on the couch in front of the television. Uncle Martin was beside her, drinking from a bottle of old cooking sherry he'd probably found in the pantry.

The swirling tufts of chest hair poking out of his dirty v-neck undershirt stored tiny remnants of food he'd consumed throughout the week.

Rachel was holding a doll that our mother and father had given her for Christmas one year over half of her face.

"Rachel," I said, "put your dolly down."

She shook her head and stole a glance at Uncle Martin, who didn't even seem to know I was there.

I walked over and gently pulled the doll to the side to uncover a shiny, swollen black eye.

I turned to Uncle Martin and snatched the bottle out of his hand, shattered it on the coffee table.

Rachel was screaming.

Martin slowly turned his head in my direction, eyelids drooping halfway down those raw, dead, bloodshot eyes of his.

He saw the jagged glass in my trembling hand. "Whatcha gon' do wittat, boy?" he drawled.

"I'm gonna make you sweat. Then I'm gonna make you cry, I don't care what it takes. I'll figure out how to do it. And then I'm gonna make you bleed."

He slapped the bottle out of my hand, slicing his fingertips open as he did so.

Fists flew, blood splattered on peeling, nicotine-caked wallpaper, and furniture was knocked over. The TV was bumped off its stand, but *Password* played on, only with Allen Ludden's head turned comically sideways.

The fight ended with Uncle Martin face down on the floor, unconscious and spreadeagled. He vomited as I carried Rachel up the stairs, and I hoped that he'd choke to death.

No such luck.

The very next evening, he was out on the porch with one of Pa's shotguns under one arm, and the bottle of Wild Turkey he'd had me get at the store under the other.

"I'm gonna get that devil," he said when I walked past him into the house after feeding the hens.

I paused, thought of a thousand replies all at once and kept them all to myself.

I went inside, and I held my sister as we listened to our father's crazy, drunken brother shoot wildly out into the night.

I wished that social worker who came by to check on us once a month woulda drove by right about then and got an eyeful of *that*.

I knew that it wouldn't be long until the land came and claimed him, though. I wanted to make its job easier, but a murder charge would only get me locked up, and I had to take care of my sister. I had to be patient. They couldn't put a cotton field on trial, but they could me.

Another week passed, and it was as bad as any of the others had been. The dogs woke me up at 3:00 AM on Tuesday, howling and barking and carrying on outside in their pens.

It was unusually warm out, and my sheets were soaked with sweat on account of there being no breeze coming in through my window. I'd been keeping it closed.

I rolled over, glanced out the window and became fully alert in half an instant.

I jumped to my feet. A hulking mass of writhing, severed human body parts and what appeared to be mud and rotting vegetation, all of it pressed together in the rough shape of a man, was lurching and stumbling across the yard, awash in the pale blue glow of the moon.

A droning chorus of stifled screams, the cries of thousands of suffering souls, rumbled deep within its bowels and escaped on its breath into the dewy night air, accompanied by the fetid stench of death. It smelled like rancid meat, and even with my window shut, the odor was overpowering enough to make my stomach churn.

It made its way over to Uncle Martin's window, and I mumbled a quick prayer, asking that he fall victim to the monster.

I wiped the fog from my breath off the glass and watched. The creature stared into the window for some time, then ran its tarry, glistening fingers over it, leaving behind streaks like snail slime.

I crept downstairs, wincing with each squeak of each step. I slipped out the front door and left it open as I wandered into the yard, towards *it*.

I stopped just five feet or so short of it.

"Get him," I said.

It turned fully around and looked at me, and I could see all of the grey, oozing, spasming components of its body very clearly. There were feet kicking, there were hands grasping at nothing, and there were eyeballs, full of confused terror, darting to and fro in an attempt to figure out where they were and what was happening.

Millipedes crawled out of gurgling mouths, trailed by black vomit. Pus bubbled beneath rotted flesh, periodically bursting out of open sores like miniature volcanoes erupting and filling the humid night air with the noxious odor of disease.

"Get him," I muttered. "C'mon, get him! We fed you all these years and we'll get back to doing it after he's gone! He's the reason you're starving!"

I don't know if it understood my words or not, but it comprehended the gist of what I was trying to convey to it.

Martin bad. Kill.

It turned back around towards the window just in time to steal a glance down the barrel of Martin's rifle.

Boom.

Shattered glass; a scream like a thousand whistling teapots.

Boom.

The creature staggered backwards, swatting at itself.

Boom.

It staggered off into the brush and disappeared into the fields.

Uncle Martin, his bare chest heaving and covered in sweat, stood holding the very same gun my father had taught me how to hunt deer with back in much happier times. Pa had taken a lot of pride in that rifle, and I hated seeing Martin's grubby, clammy hands defiling it.

"Watch and learn, boy," said Martin between labored breaths. "That's how a man defends his family."

"You're not defending anyone but yourself," I said. "It wants *you*, don't you see? Or are you too drunk to figure that out? Now I've *told* you time and time again that this land has a curse on it, and whoever tends to it must appease it with sacrifices, or else it gets tired of waiting and snatches 'em up outta their beds at night and *eats* 'em. Only reason it ain't got you yet is 'cause you wake up so easy. Maybe you should take some pills to remedy that."

He trained the barrel on me. "You watch your mouth."

"Go ahead," I said. "Shoot me. Then you'll go to prison and Rachel will get adopted by some nice family somewhere and have a normal life and forget about all this. Forget about *you*."

Martin lowered the gun and laughed. "I'm gonna wash your mouth out with turpentine," he said. "That'll teach you not to backtalk your poor old uncle."

"I'm gonna kill you."

Martin caught sight of dad's old coonhound, Betsy, wandering out of hiding, making her way towards me. He shot her, and she fell dead to the ground.

"You just try it," he said, his wicked eyes blazing with madness.

I knew, looking at him, that trying wasn't going to be good enough. Trying would get us killed.

I couldn't figure out how I was going to do him in without it looking like murder until an impulse purchase at the grocery store led to the most explosive tantrum I'd seen Uncle Martin throw yet.

He'd broken nearly all the dishes by the time he decided to clue me in on what he was so sore about.

"Peanut butter? Why'd you buy this?" He was screaming with so much force his voice cracked.

I shrugged. "Rachel likes peanut butter and jelly sandwiches. What of it?"

"*What of it?*" He chucked the jar in the trash. "I'm allergic to peanuts, that's what of it."

I had to laugh at that. Who'd ever heard of such a thing? "What happens if you eat peanuts?"

"Well, let's see," he said, scratching his chin. "I could *die*, for one thing."

"From peanuts."

"It's a real medical affliction certain folks have!" he roared. "Now you keep anything says *peanut* on it out of this house, you understand me? No peanut butter, no peanut oil, no peanut ice cream, no peanut *nothin'*!"

I nodded. He was serious. And he pronounced "oil" like my dad used to. *Awl.* I didn't like that.

The next day I went back to the store, bought a bag of peanuts and ground them up, shells and all, into a fine powder. I then poured every bit of that powder into a bottle of whiskey with a funnel and shook it. I placed the bottle next to its half-empty twin on the kitchen counter.

Wouldn't take him long to polish the other one off. Depending on his mood, it was possible he'd be breaking into the new bottle by dawn, I knew. All I had to do was be patient; wait. Play it cool.

When Uncle Martin meandered into the kitchen several minutes later to raid the refrigerator, he noticed the new bottle immediately.

"Taking a break from couch duty? Who's manning your post?" I said, which was exactly the type of thing I'd say under normal, non-murderous circumstances.

"Shaddup. Where'd that come from?"

"From the store."

"I know that, you retard. What'd you need at the store? I thought you just went."

"I forgot milk."

"I had milk on my corn flakes this morning."

He was getting suspicious. I had to steer the conversation in another direction, and fast.

"Well," I said, pretending to look sheepish, "it's just that... well there's this girl works there. Works at the checkouts. I kinda like talkin' to her, is all."

A grin slowly spread across Uncle Martin's face. The grin was ugly, just like the person behind it.

"A *girl*, huh? And here I was beginning to think you was a little fruity."

"I don't see you beatin' 'em off with a stick," I countered.

"Hey," he said, pointing at me, his thinning hair matted to his sweaty forehead, "I been with plenty of girls."

"Not smelling like *that*," I said.

For a moment it looked as if he were considering taking offense, but he just laughed and grabbed the half-empty bottle on the counter.

"I've *always* been a ladies' man. Me and your Pa, runs in the family. That's how he landed that sweet piecea tail that ended up bein' your mama."

He unscrewed the cap, tilted his head back and chugged, whiskey dripping out of the sides of his mouth.

"Real funny, Uncle Martin. You know, they say too much drinkin'll kill ya."

He ignored me and went back out into the living room, where the comforting, flickering glow of *Bonanza*, already in progress, was waiting for him with open arms.

Rachel came into the kitchen and told me she was thirsty. I poured her a glass of water with one ice cube in it, like she liked, and knelt down in front of her.

"Rachel," I said, "Uncle Martin is going to get very sick sometime either tonight or tomorrow. When that happens, I need to get him to the sweatbox, and I need you to help me fill the cans so we can feed the fields again. Whatever happens, just remember there's no reason to be scared, okay?"

She nodded, understanding. I knew she would.

The following morning, I made scrambled eggs, toast and bacon. Uncle Martin always drowned his eggs in Tabasco, and I was hoping that the spiciness of the sauce would help mask the taste of the peanuts in the whiskey, which he was sure to crack open as soon as he got up.

Sure enough, the first thing Martin did when he entered the kitchen was grab the whiskey. He slammed it down on the table and sniffed the air. "Bacon, huh? Plate me up some of that, boy."

"Yes, Uncle Martin," I said, and seconds later a heaping, steaming plate of breakfast sat in front of the horrible man who'd made it his life's work to terrorize us in the months since our Ma and Pa had passed.

It was like the last meal they used to give men about to go to the chair, except Martin didn't know he was about to die.

I had no appetite, but to keep up appearances, I shoveled forkfuls of food into my mouth as if famished.

He opened the bottle. I held my breath as he raised it to his lips, paused, and sniffed. He studied me for a moment, shrugged, then chugged.

Nothing happened.

I reasoned that it probably took a few minutes for the reaction to kick in, and I didn't panic. Uncle Martin kept eating his breakfast.

I was on the verge of losing hope when his fork suddenly clattered to the floor and he began to gasp and wheeze, clawing at his throat. I leaned forward, watching him intently.

He kicked and flailed and knocked everything off the table except his plate and the bottle, and just as I was certain that he was about to die, he stopped.

"You dumb sumbitch. Whatchu think I'm *stupid*? I didn't live this long not knowin' what peanuts smell like. I switched the bottles while you was asleep."

I thought I was about to suffer a beating for the ages, but he just snorted, scarfed down the last of his now lukewarm, rubbery eggs and took the whiskey bottle out to the living room, leaving his chair where he'd scooted it to in the middle of the kitchen upon standing up and excusing himself.

If I didn't know better, I would've thought I hurt his feelings, tryin' to kill him like that. But I do know better. Uncle Martin doesn't have any feelings. Not for anyone but himself, anyway.

After feeding all the animals that morning, I'd worked up a sweat. Sun was out early, and there wasn't a cloud in sight.

I walked out into the cracked and barren cotton fields and knelt down once I was sure I was out of sight of anyone at the house.

I rolled up my dirty shirtsleeve and took my knife out of my pocket. I pressed it to my palm, gritted my teeth, and cut my own hand open.

I cried. I cried for Rachel, and I cried for myself. I cried because I knew, finally, that we were never going to be anything. Our lives were worth spit and would only depreciate in value until they turned into something like one of those rusted-out old cars out on old man Wilkerson's property just down the road.

They weren't worth anything to anyone except young boys and girls with fertile imaginations who used to sneak through a gap in a barbed-wire fence to play cops and gangsters inside of them. Sometimes Barbara Jane (from down the lane) would come along and we'd pretend we were Bonnie and Clyde.

Yeah, that's right. I used to have friends. I used to have dreams of going someplace and being somebody. They all went and did that in the long, hard years that followed; they got out. I got left behind, somehow. I was as much a slave as the poor souls who'd been brought here in chains over one hundred years ago, doomed for all my living days, and perhaps beyond, to a life of suffering and servitude.

That's what I thought, anyway. I'd allowed myself to believe that insidious falsehood, because it was all I knew. I'd never stopped to ask why we fed the fields, and I don't know what Pa would've said if I did, because there is no good answer to that question.

If I had, though, and if he'd have answered truthfully, he'd have said, "Because we choose to, son."

It took me another four years of pouring my own life out upon that field to figure that out.

The land didn't produce anything to speak of, but I kept it bay just enough so that we could continue to suffer through our miserable lives inside of that dilapidated old depression-era farmhouse.

Martin took to beating Rachel and I eventually learned not to interfere. It was just how things were. I even talked myself into believing she deserved it, the way she went whoring around at night with boys from town, soon as she came of age.

I took to drinking, and it didn't take me long to turn into almost as big of a lush as my dear old uncle. I was turning into him, and I couldn't even see it, until one day when I hauled off and slapped Rachel across the face.

I hit her so hard she fell to the ground and as I stood over her sobbing, trembling little body, and saw the fear in her eyes, fear once reserved only for Uncle Martin, something inside me woke up.

I looked down at my calloused, dirty palm, red from the impact upon her soft, childlike flesh and curled my fingers into a fist.

No.

I wouldn't follow in *his* footsteps. And I wouldn't follow in my father's by submitting to that bloodthirsty abomination outside.

I extended my hand to help her up. She took it cautiously, but her eyes went calm as she looked into mine.

"Come on," I said. "We're leaving. Don't even pack. The devil's going to have to do his own work from now on."

Uncle Martin was passed out on the couch with a fresh piss stain on the cushion beneath him, an empty bottle of cheap bourbon at his feet. He didn't even stir when we tiptoed past and made our escape.

That was the last I ever saw of him, or the house, or of the accursed land upon which it had been built.

Rachel and I struggled for a while, but it didn't take long for me to find work and get us a place to stay. Rachel even got to go to school. She met a nice young man there, and they got married after graduation. I found a wife of my own soon after that, became a member of the Raleigh Police Force.

There were kids, grandkids, nieces and nephews. There were minivan trips to the Grand Canyon, backyard cookouts, little league games and graduation ceremonies. Joy and sorrow, laughter and tears. We learned to live.

I expect that mean old drunk got what was coming to him when the monster got hungry enough to come out of hiding again, but I don't really care one way or the other. I refuse to carry a grudge against that poor, tormented soul and live in bondage to hatred the rest of my days.

I rarely think of what life used to be like for us, back at that old farmhouse, but sometimes, on warm summer nights when I leave my bedroom window open, I can still hear a rumbling in the distance.

DANIEL & THE GRYPHON

by Christopher Allen Waldrop

On Tuesday there was a gryphon on the roof.

It was curled up sleeping and looked exactly like the picture of a gryphon from one of Daniel's books. It had the head of an eagle, but with pointed ears. It had scaly forelegs that ended in sharp talons. A pair of gray wings was folded up against its lion's body that rose and fell as it breathed deeply.

The gryphon hadn't been there the day before, which had been Daniel's first day on the roof. A few weeks earlier his mother decided he was old enough to stay alone by himself as long as he stayed in the apartment. Within a week he was exploring each floor, going up and down the stairwells. On Monday he went up one stairwell as far as it would go and opened the door to the roof. A cluster of pigeons tittered and flew away as he came out into the sun, and the pebbled surface shifted under his feet. He sat down and watched the clouds move behind the big construction cranes, wishing he'd brought a book.

That night his mother looked at the seat of his jeans and asked what he'd sat in on the playground. There had been a spot of black tar where he'd sat down, and it was sticky. Daniel just shrugged. If he told her where he'd been, his mother would make him go back to Mrs. Parker's house after school. Mrs. Parker made him go outside and play with her grandkids who were younger than Daniel unless it rained, and then she made him help her dust and mop the floors.

He walked all around the roof looking for potted plants or a pigeon coop, although he wasn't sure what one looked like, but there was no sign that anyone else ever came to the roof.

Now the gryphon was here. Daniel wondered if he should treat it like a strange dog or a wild animal, but the gryphons he'd read about could speak. He'd even read a story about a gryphon who became a schoolteacher. He sat down in front of it. The gryphon let out a low rumbling snore.

"Hello," said Daniel.

The gryphon lazily opened its eyes and raised its head.

"What is this, kid, you can't let me sleep?"

Daniel rested his chin on his hand.

"I've never seen a gryphon before."

"Well you've seen one now, so you can move along, kid."

Daniel studied the gryphon's shiny black beak.

"What do you eat?"

"You're a curious kid. All right, I eat pigeons. Sparrows. A hawk if I'm lucky. Anything I can catch on the wing."

"Do you live here?"

"Just passing through. It's a stop on my, what do you call it, migratory route."

Daniel looked at the gryphon's long black tail that ended in a point like an arrowhead.

"Where do you come from?"

"Kid, I've flown across the lands and waters since before they had names, and the names they do have keep changing. When I'm ready I'll fly into the sunset."

"It's almost the summer solstice. After that the days will get shorter all the way to the middle of winter." Daniel was very proud of himself for knowing this. "Well, it was nice meeting you," he went on, getting up, "but my mom will be home soon. I need to be there because I'm not allowed out when she's not around."

"Mm hmm." The gryphon put its head back down and closed its eyes.

After he got back to the apartment his mom called to say she'd be late and that Daniel should make himself some supper. He heated two hot dogs in the microwave for two minutes and twenty-two seconds. The microwave wasn't that old but only the numbers on the middle row of the keypad still worked.

"Nothing's built to last anymore," was his mother's response, which made Daniel think of his dad. When Daniel couldn't sleep his dad would come and sit next to his bed. His dad's silhouette was comforting, a something darkness in the nothing darkness of the room.

For Daniel's ninth birthday his dad gave him an old watch.

"My dad gave me this to keep me company in the dark," he said. "You hear that ticking? That's how you know it's always with you."

Daniel had only seen his grandfather, who lived in another state, a few times, but he thought about how the watch connected him to his dad and to his grandfather, the way the sun connected the planets.

When Daniel's dad died his mother said something popped inside his head like a balloon. No one knew. His dad thought he just had a headache that day, and the doctors couldn't do anything to help even after he'd been rushed to the hospital. Daniel kept the watch next to his bed where it would sometimes reflect the moonlight, and he'd lie in bed listening to it tick until dreamless sleep made everything silent.

When his mom got home she lugged a box with a new microwave into the apartment. The old microwave was black, and its numbers glowed a soft green. The new one was silver, and the numbers were a harsh bright blue even with the kitchen lights on. Daniel wished they could just keep the old microwave as long as it still worked.

The toilet screamed when his mom flushed it. It kept screaming until it was filled again.

"How long has it been doing that?" his mother asked.

Daniel shrugged. It had started making that sound only that afternoon, and the sound could be heard through the whole apartment.

"Naturally. I fix one thing, and something else breaks. It's probably just air in the pipes but I'll call the super and have him send the plumber anyway." His mother sighed as she went through the mail. "And the rent's going up again. Can you stay home tomorrow?"

"School's almost over." Daniel didn't think the noise the toilet made was hurting anything and that fixing it could wait.

"Okay, but tomorrow you come straight home, and no lollygagging anywhere."

On Wednesday the gryphon was in the same spot. Daniel sat down in front of it.

"Hello."

The gryphon opened its eyes and raised its head.

"Oh, hey, kid."

"How old are you?"

The gryphon blinked. "Why would I keep track?"

"I'm about to turn ten." Daniel had thought a lot about this. His age would never be measured in single digits again. It was a big change, but no one he knew seemed to think there was anything special about it.

"Ten summers and ten winters," said the gryphon.

Daniel put his chin on his hand. "If I brought some corn and scattered it around so pigeons would come here would you like that?"

"I catch most of my food in flight."

"Okay." Daniel stood up. "I have to go because we might have the plumber coming."

The plumber was at the door of the apartment. He was a big man with a bag of tools. He smiled brightly as Daniel came down the hall.

"Hullo. Are you the master of the house?"

Daniel wasn't sure about this, but he said, "I'm sorry if you've been waiting."

"It's okay. I just got here."

As Daniel opened the door the plumber said, "I'm Phil. What's your name?"

"Daniel."

"All right Danny, and what's the trouble today?"

As he was showing the plumber to the bathroom Daniel asked if he'd ever seen the gryphon.

"Griffin? Yeah, I think I know Griffin. He does the electrical work, don't he?"

Daniel didn't know what to say to this, so he watched the plumber flush the toilet. Over the screaming the plumber said, "Faulty fill valve. We'll get this fixed in no time."

He went to the linen closet and adjusted something then flushed the toilet again. Daniel watched as he took the lid off and pulled out parts, replacing them with new ones.

"You think you wanna be a plumber when you grow up?"

"No." Daniel didn't know what he wanted to be when he grew up, and he hated the question. Sometimes he wished everything could just stop.

After the plumber left the toilet didn't scream anymore. There was just the rush of water, the hiss as it refilled, and too much silence after.

On Thursday the gryphon was already up and looking toward him when Daniel opened the door to the roof.

Because school was ending Daniel helped clean the classroom that day. He had changed schools in March after he and his mother moved. His new class was right in the middle of a unit on the planets and building a solar system that stretched across the room. Everyone else had already been sorted into groups and given planets to paint. The teacher gave him a small white ball and told him since Pluto was the smallest planet he could work on it by himself.

"Can I have a smaller ball to make Charon?" he asked. "And if you have another I could make Eris. It's bigger than Pluto."

The teacher smiled and said, "That's okay, hon. We're just working on the planets."

Daniel wanted to tell her Pluto was no longer considered a planet, but she had already turned to tell the group painting Jupiter to not make it so messy.

Now they had to get rid of it all.

He helped the other students take down the large papier-mâché sun at one end of the room and felt a twinge of annoyance as Mercury, Venus, Earth, and Mars were grabbed and casually tossed in the garbage.

While a group of boys gathered around the sun and started tearing it into pieces Daniel went to find the model of Pluto he'd painted red and brown, with its big heart-shaped white spot, but someone had already thrown it away.

"Hello," said Daniel after he sat down in front of the gryphon. It grunted and gave one ear a quick scratch with its back leg.

"I ate a Canadian goose today, and it's sitting really heavy on my stomach," the gryphon said.

Daniel had seen Canadian geese in the park. They were very smart looking but were mean and hissed at him. His mom told him to stay away from them because they could hurt him badly. He was glad the gryphon had gotten one.

"Did you catch it while flying?"

"On the ground. I got a nest full of goslings too, and I needed that. I have a big day ahead of me tomorrow."

"Tomorrow's a big day for me too. Tomorrow is the end of school." Daniel thought for a minute. "I don't know what will happen after that. Maybe I'll go back to Mrs. Parker's or something. We didn't live here last summer, and I don't think my mom will want me to spend all day in the apartment. Everybody else is excited about the summer, but I kind of want to stay in school where I know things."

The gryphon looked out over the skyline.

"I almost flew into one of those cranes chasing a sparrow today, and there are buildings that weren't there when I came this way a year ago. What is it with you people and changing? The sun rises and sets, the waters move, forests grow and fall, the seasons change. Isn't that enough for you?"

"My mom says we might have to move because of all the new construction. That means I might have to change schools again. She says I need to be prepared, but I really don't want to go. I didn't want to leave our house, but now I like it here. Nobody else has to move like we do."

The gryphon stood up and stretched.

"I'm gonna go over to the shade and sleep. See you later, kid." It walked around to the other side of the roof where Daniel couldn't see it.

On Friday the gryphon wasn't there.

That day was the end-of-year assembly at school. Daniel stood next to Michael, the only friend he'd made. He'd had friends at his other school, but they were too far away now.

"I'll call you next week," Michael told him. "We can hang out. Maybe you can come to the pool with me. That's what we did last summer. My mom spends all day sitting next to the pool, and I swim."

Daniel didn't want to admit he didn't know how to swim.

"I have a birthday in two weeks."

Michael brightened. "You have a birthday in the summer? That's so cool. Mine is in January, right after New Year's. My mom says just thinking about it makes her tired."

Michael kept talking about things they could do all through the assembly while grownups took turns giving speeches about accomplishments and looking to the future. Daniel thought all Michael's ideas sounded great since his mom would be at work.

He thought the gryphon might be out eating birds, so he sat on the roof, carefully avoiding any tar, and waited. He opened his backpack, took out some paper, and started to draw a picture of the gryphon in flight. He hoped it would like it.

After an hour he went back downstairs.

On Saturday his mom had to go to work for a few hours in the morning. Daniel ran up to the roof as soon as she left, but the gryphon wasn't there.

On Sunday after church his mom let him go to the store one block over to get some ice cream. He went to the roof first, but the gryphon wasn't there.

On Monday Daniel stayed alone in the apartment. His mom apologized for not planning something; she'd been so busy summer had just crept up on her, and she'd work out a place for him to go before his birthday.

He wondered if Michael would ever call. He made several trips to the roof. The gryphon wasn't there, and Daniel didn't linger in case the phone rang.

Tuesday afternoon Daniel spent a long time on the roof. The air was hot and thick. A blanket of clouds crossed over the sun and thunder rumbled. Daniel stayed close to the door and only went inside when fat raindrops started to fall, darkening the roof.

The phone was ringing when he got to the apartment.

"Where were you?" his mom demanded.

"In the bathroom."

"I called an hour ago. Have you been in the bathroom that long?"

"I forgot to call back."

His mom sighed. "Boy, sometimes I worry about you." She paused. "I'm going to stop and pick up a pizza after work. How does that sound?"

Pizza sounded good, but after he hung up Daniel wondered if it meant something. Sometimes his mom brought home pizza just because or if she worked late several days in a row, but she'd brought home pizza the day his dad died and when she told him they were going to have to move.

Daniel ran up to the roof. The storm had passed and in the low places where the pebbles had been pushed aside puddles shone brightly. A cluster of pigeons tittered and flew away as he went to the edge. He climbed up and stretched out his arms like he could fly into the setting sun.

THE SEASIDE LOLLY SHOP

by Mark Towse

There was no advertising, nothing in the papers, or even online to indicate that the town would be host to a new lolly shop. Over the last few days, the builders had been in—working around the clock. No sign of the owners yet.

"I can't wait. I just can't wait," Zac said excitedly to Ryan. "It's going to be amazing."

And Ryan had to agree.

From the outside, it looked like any other shop, but through the window, it was like a scene from a fairy tale—a cavern of delights bursting with color and the promise of flavor beyond anything already experienced. The corner of Cameo Drive and Petunia Street had just become their new favorite place.

"Two hours, and it's all ours!" Zac shouted, and the candy-induced excess saliva from his mouth sprayed across the window.

"Dude! That's gross." And they both laughed.

The last of the tourists left on Friday—holiday season over, and the town had already settled into a more relaxed place. The stress in the resident's faces was slowly fading, and once again, they could enjoy their seaside dwellings without the hordes of disillusioned adults and spoilt kids.

"Don't you ever get sick of it, Ry?" Zac asked seriously. "The tourists."

"What do you mean?" Ryan replied.

"We never get to go anywhere — Christ, I've not even been out of town, have you?"

"You know I haven't. But we live in a holiday spot, Z. Most people would be jealous that we get to spend our time here."

"True. But we never get to enjoy the best of it without the crowds," Zac said, kicking a pebble across the street. "It's a big world out there, Ry. Every time I mention it, my parents say it's the busiest time for us — can't afford to leave during the silly season blah, blah, blah. I'm sick of it — it doesn't seem fair that we miss out."

"I guess it makes sense, though, Z. Most people around here run shops or café's or hotels."

"I know that," Zac replied, "but nobody ever seems to go anywhere — apart from the church and the endless community meetings — I don't even know what the oldies find to talk about for all that time!"

"I think that's the same in most towns, Z. Most tourists are probably jealous that we get to spend our time here."

"But aren't you bored? I am. I'm not staying here a second longer than I need to. Everyone is the same — it's like you can set your clock by them."

"I guess. But my dad said he loves this town. He said that everyone does, and that's why nobody leaves," Ryan said.

"Nobody leaves," Zac repeated menacingly and ran his finger across his neck.

Ryan laughed and shook his head, but he felt differently than Zac. He enjoyed the feeling of a small community and the safety it promised. Every night on television, there were reports of murder and suicide in other towns — it seemed to be getting worse all the time. Much worse.

The sign on the shop door read: *Open 8 am Sunday. Don't forget your pocket money!*

"My dad said they are crazy opening just after the holiday season. It doesn't make any sense," Ryan said.

"And 8 am on a Sunday?" Zac offered.

They finally pulled themselves away from the window and headed to the beach.

"Anyway, who cares, at least we won't have to fight our way to the good stuff," Zac smiled.

"I hope they have those gobstoppers that last for ages!"

"Me too. Might get some peace around here!" Ryan shouted, before giving Zac a sharp punch on the arm, and sprinting off towards the sand.

As if on cue for the post-holiday season, the clouds had rolled in overnight and blocked out any sun. Ryan always thought the sea looked unhappy once the people left, and today was no exception. Say what you want about the tourists, but they brought energy — life to the place. Greyish water frothed in the distance and matched the color of the sky, and the sand now looked more bronze than gold. Everything looked less vibrant, like washed-out images from the old movies his dad sometimes watched.

There was nobody else on the beach, and they made the most it — hurling mud cakes at each other, chasing each other around, and playing chicken with the water.

"What time is it now?" Zac asked.

"Five thirty-two! What the hell did you want to get up so early for anyhow?"

"I don't know," Zac replied. "I guess it's like Christmas — you know, the excitement, the anticipation. It's the most exciting thing that has happened in this town since — well, forever. Besides, I've never been allowed out my room before six. We are twelve now, and we have rules to break!"

"I need new friends," Ryan sighed, shaking his head.

Both stared at the water, and for a moment, both were silent.

"You know what's weird, Ry?"

"Yeah, you!"

"No. I'm serious. It sounds nuts, but sometimes I can hear the water calling my name. And — and I have this — "

"Urge to go in?" Ryan interrupted.

Zac turned to him, "Yeah! Do you feel it too?"

"No. It's just you, you weirdo!" he replied, laughing nervously. But he did, and it scared him. Sometimes he woke up in the middle of the night with the feeling that he was choking on the cold salt-water—hacking up dry air and covered in his damp salty sweat. His mum said that he would soon grow out of it.

They looked back out towards the water, and almost in unison, the hair on the back of their necks began to prickle. Both felt it, not just the pull—something else, too—a gentle vibration that sat at the base of their spine, accompanied by a low and almost indiscernible hum.

"Do you see that? Over there, just to the right." Zac said, breaking the spell.

"No, where are you—oh, shit. What is that?" Ryan replied with a question.

It was too far out to see clearly, but it wasn't a trick of the light or the turn of a wave. The water was as flat as an ice-rink, apart from a dozen or so spherical swirls of mist that hovered over the grey.

A sudden and gentle breeze brushed across them and brought with it a pungent smell. To Zac, it smelt like someone had just crapped a ton of seaweed.

"Mate, you could have waited," Zac remarked, trying to lighten the atmosphere.

But they both picked up on it. The sun was up there somewhere, but the morning was quickly growing darker and colder, as though regressing towards midnight. And as they stood there watching, the waves began to grow and as their hair ruffled in the increasing wind, both of their stomachs developed a knot and the hairs on their necks continued to send their warning signals.

"Race you back!" Zac said and returned the blow to the arm.

And they ran in fear. But would never admit that to each other.

Even the fairground — their newly delegated second favorite place — became a temporary source of alarm as they sprinted past the big wheel — its carriages rocking gently on their rusty hinges in the impromptu wind.

Neither of them turned around as they ran nervously back towards the shopfront, and relief swept across both when the huge glass window came into view. For now, candy was back on their mind, and whatever happened at the beach could stay there.

"I'm gonna eat 'til I chuck!" Ryan spluttered.

And here, the air was okay again — the faint smell of seaweed but nothing as putrid as it was near the water. The wind ceased almost instantly, and the morning light quickly returned.

"What the hell are we going to do for the next two hours?" Ryan asked, shoulders bobbing up and down as he sucked in air.

"I don't know, Ry. Should we go back home and come back later?"

"So, we got up at 5.30 am for a romantic stroll on the beach! People will talk, Z. Nah, I reckon we stay here — perhaps they will open early. They might even give us some free stuff as the first customers."

"And I'm Donald Trump!" Zac exclaimed.

"You are many things," Ryan said, "but you will never sink that low."

The chances of them being out of bed this early during the holidays would have ordinarily been zero, but both were banned from their iPads before the holiday even started. At school, Jeremy Fraser had given them a link to some extremely adult material, and at such a very early stage in their pornographic journey, it had shocked both—possibly damaged them for life. Neither enjoyed what they saw, but of course, they would never admit that. The only thing they both admitted was how silly they had been to not delete their browser history.

"I've got a game we can play," Zac said. And with that, he removed two coins from his pocket and gave one to Ryan. "You have to flick it towards the wall, and the closest one wins."

Ryan looked at him and frowned, "Right. Sorry, could you explain that one again? I thought, for a moment, you said we are going to throw coins at a wall for the next two hours."

"Just try it!"

And for the next few minutes, they threw coins at a wall.

"Z, you smell that?"

"Yeah. Seaweed again."

But it was stronger than that, and they knew it—the same festering smell that had made them both queasy on the beach was returning with a vengeance.

"Z, down the street," Ryan nodded.

And Zac turned, "What?"

"Over there—the mist."

Zac scanned the road again until finally, he saw the vapor gradually making its way towards them. It was a surreal and eerie vision that sent both Zac and Ryan behind the wall of the shop.

"Creepy," they said in unison but didn't laugh.

The mist was heading straight for them, and the closer it got, the more they shrunk into each other, afraid that, if seen, it might devour them both.

Soon, a sporadic low humming accompanied its approach, and they felt the noise vibrate through their bodies, as though they were connected in some way to the surreal turn of events.

And just when Zac was about to ask what it was, the mist began to separate. Wisps of cloud swirled viciously around, still adjoined but with much more independence, and they darted into two new formations that resembled—

"Shit, no way," Ryan whispered.

Humans.

The smell was intense—the sort that would linger in the nostrils for long afterwards. As would the vision of the approaching forms.

Frozen, they continued to observe from behind the wall.

"I wish I was still in bed," Zac murmured.

The vibration within them was more intense. "Can you feel it, Zac?"

He nodded.

It ran up their spine, a quick rhythm of pulses that wasn't painful, just unnerving in a way that an external force could create such a strong internal reaction. The mist became more solid as the shapes approached. It became busier, too—more purposeful and methodical in its movement. The shapes were soon without gaps, dense gaseous forms that moved in harmony in a human-like way—walking, with makeshift shoulders gently oscillating.

"Have you got your phone, Z?" Ryan asked, reaching his hand urgently towards Zac.

"No, it's on my bedside table."

"Damn, I left mine too!"

As the shapes continued to approach, the smell became even fouler—almost unbearable—and both had their hands across their mouths and nostrils. The human clouds were now only a few feet away from the shop, and the menacing hum and vibration they brought were getting more intense.

Zac wanted to block his ears too—to drown out the noise. His heart was pumping fast, and he knew he was approaching his limit—this wasn't fun to him—he didn't enjoy fear. He thought about making a run for it but didn't think his legs would work.

Ryan showed no intention of leaving, but the thought had certainly crossed his mind. Instead, he put his arm around his friend's shoulder and a finger to his mouth.

Finally, the mist began to shroud the front of the shop, until the window was completely covered, and then it slowly started to seep under the door. The event wasn't a freak of nature—some random physical reaction—it was intentional and terrifying.

Neither of them dared to breathe as they watched the last of the mist slip under the door, and only when they were sure it had completely dispersed, did they sneak back around to the front window.

As they both peered through the bottom of the glass and beyond the many jars of jellies, they witnessed the mist slowly start to break down—little clouds at a time floating away and quickly dissipating. Something was being revealed—the gaseous cloak was being removed.

Both terrified but unable to turn away, they continued to watch the entire show, eyes wide and mouths open. The first glimpse of skin appeared—an arm—but that soon gave way to more, and slowly but surely the mist continued to lift until impossibly in front of their very eyes, there now stood two regular old people—naked—each of their faces dominated by two pitch-black eyes.

The man was chubby with grey hair and a rather small penis. The woman was also quite round with long white hair and saggy breasts that pointed towards the ground. It was impossible to see her bits underneath the excess flesh.

It was the black eyes that sparked fear in both Ryan and Zac. Apart from that, they looked perfectly human. Like some cheap trick, they had once been a wall of fog—but there were no hidden cameras or mirrors—the boys had witnessed real magic.

The old man looked around the shop and nodded to himself, seemingly happy with his lot. He then took the hand of the old lady, and they began to dance jovially around the shop. The eyes had changed too now—humanized—the transformation complete.

Zac and Ryan looked at each other to make sure they were both seeing the same thing.

The stench was gone and replaced by the familiar and relatively innocent smell of their seaside home. But they knew it would never be the same again.

"We are going to go home, and we are going to talk about this later. I don't think I am feeling candy for today," Ryan stated as he checked his watch. 6 am.

"Should we say anything, Ryan?"

"What the hell would we say? And who would we tell? My parents wouldn't be happy if they knew I was out and about at this time. I'm already banned from my iPad — I don't want to get grounded!" Ryan replied.

"Yeah, but what the fuck just happened, Ry?"

"Mate, I have no idea. One thing is for sure, though. I'm off candy."

"Me too," Zac said. "This is all too weird."

"Agreed. Look, let's go back home for a bit — check in and meet up later."

"I think I choose boredom," Zac said.

And with that, they went home, crept back into their beds, and pretended there was a rational explanation to what they had just seen.

But neither of them could get the episode out of their minds — messaging each other relentlessly about their theories, without arriving at anything that remotely made sense. Zac kept thinking he could see little wisps of mist through his bedroom window. There was no doubt it had him spooked. The smell was still with him, too — one of those that lingered in the nostrils for hours afterward.

Both swore not to say anything to their parents — this was their mystery to solve. Who were these mysterious people from the sea, and why the hell did they buy a lolly shop?

7.55 am. They met at the top of Barley Street as arranged, one street down from Cameo Drive where the lolly shop was located. Already the queue of children lining up was at least forty deep, and others were joining. They knew everyone in line—all of them incredibly animated, most likely a combination of the chilly morning and the anticipation of exchanging their easy come by pocket money for as much candy as it would buy. Some of their parents were chatting in the line or in little groups that had splintered off. Even they looked happy—most likely relieved that the lolly shop had finally opened and would put an end to the whiny anticipation from their offspring.

And then the door opened, and the little bell rang.

Both Ryan and Zac tried to get a good look at the owners, but the first customers were quickly rushed in—perhaps only three of the kids—and the door closed behind them.

"What—" Zac announced.

"It's so nobody nicks the candy," Ryan said.

"What if they don't come back out?" Zac asked.

"I don't think they would do anything, not in front of all these witnesses," Ryan replied.

A couple of minutes later, three children came out, each carrying a lumpy white paper bag and wearing a smile from ear to ear. They approached Zac and Ryan, each comparing their bounty and the order in which they were going to consume the candy. Out of the group of them, Tim was the first to look up from his stash and notice the two boys loitering.

"What are you guys up to?" he said as he pushed his spectacles back up his nose.

"I wouldn't eat them if I were you," Zac warned

The three of them looked at him as though Zac had just told them that potatoes grow on trees.

"Are you ill, Zac?" Sarah suggested. The group of three laughed in unison and continued down the street.

"Do you think they're going to poison the town?" Ryan said to him.

"Maybe the kids. Who knows?"

They continued to watch as the routine continued — one group in, and one out — sometimes two kids, but never more than three at a time. Zac and Ryan watched vigilantly for any unusual behavior from the children as they crammed in as much chocolate and jellies as would fit into their sugar hungry mouths. But they only made themselves jealous, stomachs growling and mouths watering as each of the happy customers brought out impossibly colorful candy from their contrasting stark white receptacle.

Finally, the line outside the shop disappeared, and the town was once again, devoid of life — almost back to normal.

Almost.

"We have to go in," Ryan said. "We have to see."

"See what?" Zac replied half-heartedly but knew it was inevitable.

"Nobody is going to believe what we saw. We need proof. You know that, Z."

A minute's silence followed, as though marking the end to their childhood — they could be heroes or killed in action. And finally, they began their slow walk towards the corner of Cameo Drive, each of them hoping the other might come up with a reasonable excuse to back out.

The colors only seemed to get brighter as they approached the shop front—shiny assortments of reds, yellows, blues and greens, and other colors they could not find a name for—ones that seemed other-worldly almost. They knew they would not be able to eat the candy, not after what they had seen.

As they stood outside the shop deliberating, they realized that they had no real plan, but before they could even think of retreating, the door opened, and the chime sang.

The woman stood there in a yellow floral dress, full face of makeup, and wearing a smile that looked perfectly warm and friendly. There were no signs to indicate her recent emergence from the sea—no gills, no seaweed in the hair, or fins. She just looked like a fat old lady.

"Well come on in then! Don't just stand there like you've just been caught playing with yourself."

They looked at each other and entered the shop. The place was a heady cocktail of chocolate and candy that you could almost taste—no hint of rotting seaweed. The woman smiled and gestured towards the white paper bags. Ryan was the first to grab one and begin to fill it with an assortment of soft and hard jellies. Zac followed suit warily, occasionally glancing back to the old lady in case she turned into a cloud.

"Do you boys like licorice?" she said.

Ryan eyed Zac again before giving a quick nod.

The lady hobbled over to a large jar filled to the brim with licorice and removed two pieces. "Here, these are on the house," she said and held them out.

"Th—Thanks," Zac said and noted the perfectly human hands as he reached for his stick of licorice.

"Morning, boys!" the cheerful voice boomed from behind them.

They both turned in alarm to see the old man sporting khaki shorts and a Hawaiian T-shirt, not the typical winter wardrobe you would expect, especially for an oldie.

"Morning," they both said meekly in unison and began to back away slowly towards the door.

"Aren't you forgetting something?" the man said.

"Th-Thanks," Ryan spluttered.

"To pay! Silly sausage!"

"Oh yeah—sorry."

And the owners began to laugh; gently at first, but it slowly became louder and more guttural until they were both doubled over and coughing and spluttering—shoulders heaving up and down like heavy machinery and eyes so red they looked as though they might pop.

"On the house. But don't let your shadow scare you on the way home!" the old man shouted.

Zac was first to the door and pushed himself through as quickly as possible. Ryan followed closely behind, but just as he was about to let the door go, he turned to see the old man and woman standing together, hand in hand, and eyes as black as the licorice they had been sold.

He shut the door and launched into a speed walk.

"Zac…"

"What? Hang on, wait for me."

"Their eyes. Don't look back, but they turned black. Like before."

"Are you sure?"

"Zac, I'm sure."

"What's going on, Ryan?"

And Ryan turned back towards him and simultaneously raised his shoulders and eyebrows.

Back to the relative safety of Barley Street, they began to rifle through their colorful haul.

"We can't eat this, can we, Z?"

Ryan acknowledged his friend's obvious disappointment. Never take candy from strangers was the rule when he was younger, and he imagined that would be even more applicable for those that came from the sea with eyes like black marbles.

"No," Zac replied. He, too, felt a pang of sadness as he peered into the color filled paper bag. "We'll have to wait. See if it's safe."

They made a pact not to eat even one, and then spent most of the day together searching for theories on their iPads. They came up with nothing they could label as credible, or that wasn't written by some nutcase with a host of other conspiracy theories. But then again, how could anything be dismissed after what they had seen.

"Let's meet in the morning, 5.30 am sharp, on the beach — and bring your phone so we can get photos," Zac said.

They high-fived and made their way home.

Ryan kept checking the bag of candy — he didn't really pay much attention when in the shop. As soon as he had entered, he wanted to get out, so he had quickly scooped the first things he saw. They looked normal. In fact, no, they looked perfect — so smooth and shiny. The scent from the bag was delicious too, mouthwateringly so — but they had a deal, and besides, he didn't want to spend his days as a puff of smoke.

Both his parents were waiting for him at the kitchen table. "Ryan!" his mum shouted enthusiastically as soon as he had stepped through the back door — a huge smile planted across her face.

"Hi," he said as he carried on walking.

"So?" his parents said simultaneously — expectant looks across both faces.

"So?" he echoed.

"The candy," his Dad said, pointing towards the bag, "I thought you would have eaten it all by now?"

"No, I'm—saving them—for later. Why?"

"How can you do that?" his mum said dramatically. "Look at the colors. Which one did you try?" she sang—her face a map of inquisitiveness. "You did eat one, didn't you?" she fired again urgently. And with that, her face became sharper—a series of more serious lines.

He studied both of his parents, and they emanated the same anxious demeanor: arms folded and leaning in towards him. The jovial greeting seemed like a distant memory.

"Are you guys okay?" Ryan asked.

"Ryan, try the red ones. They are out of this world, mate," his dad suggested.

"I—I had a blue one already," he lied and watched the relief wash over them as he backed away towards the stairs.

Shutting the door to his room, he grabbed his phone from his desk and threw himself onto the bed. Something was off. What was that downstairs? He texted Zac and found he had the same ordeal—an abnormal interest in the candy he had chosen and whether he had eaten any. Of course, to get them off his back, Zac had also lied to his parents and said he had eaten some.

They both spent the rest of the evening in their rooms texting each other. Ryan only went down for dinner, sitting through an awkward and extended period of intense paranoia. Bedtime could not come fast enough for him. He had so many questions, and tomorrow would hopefully bring some clarity. He rested his head on the pillow and pictured their photographs in the paper—headline: local boys stop an alien takeover of a small seaside town. And he realized how silly he was being and closed his eyes.

He woke at 4 am, before the alarm even had a chance—heart thumping and covered in sweat—another nightmare. Standing on the beach, the cloud of fog had surrounded him and slowly closed in until he could see only grey. It had a pressure that was light at first, but that gradually began to build until he could feel it compressing his chest, legs, and face—and then it had intensified so quickly until he thought his skull and ribcage might shatter. Then he was awake. The cloud had gone, but he still felt something—a malevolence—as though he had brought it back into the real world. And there was that faint smell of rotting seaweed—or whatever that now familiar rancid odor was.

Peeling the sheets away, he walked over to the window and looked down towards the dark street below. He shivered—not just the cold, but something didn't feel right—there was an undertone around town. Perhaps it was all in his imagination—too many late-night movies on his iPad. But he was going to find out. That slow humming was back too; he could feel its distant rhythm and the ever so slight vibration down his spine.

It was over an hour until he was due to meet Zac, and he wasn't sure if he could wait that long. He dressed, picked up his phone, and stealthily tip-toed into the hallway, holding his breath as he reached his parent's room. The snoring that emanated was soothing at first, but he soon realized the patterns were repeating as if an audio recording on a loop.

Even more sinister, was how in time the bursts were with the gentle tremors that rippled through his body.

There was a torch in his Dad's bedside table. He remembered from the night he heard something in the roof, and it turned out to be a bird.

If he could slip in and out and quickly grab it.

His eyes were growing used to the dark, and the opaqueness was giving way to more defined shapes. As soon as he pushed the already ajar door to his parent's room further inwards, he saw the outline of their faces, both facing the ceiling, eyes closed but mouths wide open — the same deep snore simultaneously emitting from both. He crept closer to his mum's bedside and moved his face towards hers. The noise and lack of movement appeared so robotic. She laid perfectly still — no twitching, no facial movement whatsoever — as if nobody was home. He moved across to his dad's side, but it was the same. They looked lifeless.

What the fuck.

"Dad!" he whispered into his ear. Nothing.

"Dad!" he said more urgently and louder. Still nothing.

And in desperation, he shouted this time, "DAD!" and planted his hands into his father's shoulders, rocking him up and down against the mattress. His head lolloped against the pillow, eventually falling to the side, and the guttural throat noises continued.

There was a knot developing in Ryan's stomach now — this no longer seemed like an adventure but something far more sinister. His ear began to pulsate loudly in time with his heart, and that damn humming — barely audible but certainly there and beginning to drive him crazy.

Somehow, he knew it was all connected.

He grabbed the torch from the drawer and slowly started to back away, willing for some spark of life, but they just lay there like rag dolls, and he was glad to be putting distance between them.

Downstairs, it was cold and dark, and he found himself on the verge of tears, longing for the time before the sweetshop appeared — when his innocence was intact — or perhaps ignorance. He sat at the kitchen table, trying to piece it all together. But this wasn't CSI — this was a whole new ballgame — the mist, the strange people from the sea, the lolly shop, and the humming.

He picked up his phone with only the intention of killing more time. After trying a few more searches, he found nothing interesting — plenty of coverage of other local businesses but not a single mention of the new lolly shop.

5 am, and he could wait no longer. He grabbed the torch and gently let the door close, mindful that it would be unlikely to wake his parents from their incredibly deep sleep.

It was getting chilly as he approached the beach, and he began to see clouds of breath in front of him that made him immediately nervous. The sea looked thick and dark, like a congealed soup that had been left out overnight. It was completely flat again, not even a ripple. 5.05 am. He sat down with arms folded across his legs and blew his little smoke rings while trying to ignore the deep hum that continued to torment. The water gently faded away into foam on the sand, but it was slowly creeping closer to his feet each time. And that feeling hit him again of wanting to surrender to the water — it felt like a wave washing over him and dragging him out to sea — the pull was undeniable. He planted his heels firmly into the sand, afraid that it just might be possible. The growing intensity of the vibration through his bones could not be ignored either.

The beach was the root of it all — he knew that now.

And just as he could take no more, sat in the dark, terrified, and longing for normality, he spotted the first of the balls of mist hovering above the dark water. 5.28 am. And as if on cue the smell that started to make itself known, lodging at the back of his throat.

Come on, Zac. Where are you?

As he reached for his phone, he felt the first touch of wind on his face, and he vigorously shivered. His fingers continued to shake as he typed the text to Zac, *Wakey, wakey, where are you, dude?*

And then the first ripples on the water began — it was happening again. More of the spheres of mist developed but appeared undisturbed by the wind that now whistled through. They started to draw closer, moving in unison towards the shore and only temporarily visible between the waves that were developing.

Zac, I'm gonna kill you. 5.29 am.

He started to edge slowly away, urgently turning back and forth to see if his friend was coming but also to keep an eye on the nearing clusters. There were far too many to count now, and more emerging from behind. And as each wave disappeared, the fragments of fog closed in, and the humming picked up further momentum.

Enough was enough.

And Ryan ran for it — the sound of his feet pounding against the sand could only just be heard over the rattling wind and the large waves that now crashed behind him. A quick look around and some of the shapes were almost out of the water — clusters of mist that swirled and floated ethereally towards him.

He ran for his life.

And as he sprinted towards Cameo Drive, the wind began to drop — the panic, for now, was easing. He dropped his pace to a gentle jog and took in some deep breaths. In the distance, he could see the lolly shop, but no sign of his friend and the phone still showed no missed calls or texts. He could only assume Zac had slept in.

The window of the shop was still in relative darkness, but the 'Premises for sale' sign was clearly visible in the top right-hand corner. Even before he reached the shop-front, he knew the contents would be cleared out. And he was right — the place was deserted.

5.40 am. He leaned against the shop window to get his breath back, squinting through the glass just in case he caught a glimpse of the strangers.

Finally, as he turned his head away and back towards the street, his legs turned to jelly, and he desperately let his head rest against the glass window for support.

There were clouds of fog everywhere.

They moved with purpose and in intentional directions — a menacing scene of alien life visiting their small coastal town. Ryan remained pinned against the shop front, terrified to move — terrified to breathe. Surely, they could see him.

The fog continued to drift, seemingly oblivious to Ryan's presence. Zac's house was only a couple of minutes away if he could reach it. He slowly edged forwards, trying to remain as silent as possible — he would wait for a suitable gap and make a run for it. Over there — a space. And he took his chances and ran as fast as he could. His heart was in his mouth as he ran, his head constantly flicking around to see if he was being chased.

He didn't have a chance — the large cloud appeared from around the corner of Zac's street. And running straight through it, he prepared for the worst — the nightmare images of it seeping into his mouth and turning his soul black flashed before him. He couldn't face that.

But there was no reaction — the patch of mist merely continued to float in the opposite direction.

He felt unchanged.

As he nervously made his way down Zac's street, he got behind another small procession, still wary of being too exposed. He observed as it began to break up into smaller groups and then smaller again. The individual shapes veered off in different directions until there were only a few forms ahead of Ryan. Finally, his friend's house was only a few meters ahead — but it didn't look anywhere near as welcoming as it did in daylight. As he stepped out from the group, one of the shapes also stepped out, and he anxiously watched as it floated ahead of him towards Zac's house.

5.50 am.

The mist started to seep through his friend's front door.

Although apparently unconcerned or unaware of his presence, it did not stop Ryan feeling terrified about what was unfolding in front of him. He pressed his face against the upper glass of the frame as the mist continued to disseminate under the front door, and through any other gaps that it could force its way into. Within a matter of seconds, the last of it had made its way through, and the formation on the other side suddenly began to swirl violently like a tornado — fragments of the cloud breaking off and disappearing, and then — no way — the first patch of human-like skin was revealed. As it continued to disperse, the shape finally began to take form, and within seconds, Ryan was left staring at the naked backside of his best friend's mum.

For a moment, she stood there as if in a trance, until finally, she began to walk casually up the stairs.

From the corner of his eye, he saw more mist arriving at the window, and he peeled himself away to watch as it began to feed itself through the door. Nose straight back to the window, he observed the same aggressive spiraling of the cloud and the gradual splintering of the outer mist. He prayed that it was Zac's father in there, but slowly as the mist cleared, the skin started to become visible. A warm tear began to trickle down his left cheek with the realization that he was looking at his best friend. On the third step, Zac turned, and his black eyes stared directly into Ryan's. They stayed like that for a while in a sinister stand-off before Zac turned and made his way upstairs towards his inanimate doppelgänger.

Ryan backed away from the door—a feeling of intense loneliness and confusion.

He realized what had happened. He should have taken Zac's bag, too—he knew what he was like—probably just thought one would be okay.

The mist had cleared from the streets—not a single wisp remained.

6 am.

The streetlights started to flicker on, but the dirty halogen light did nothing to raise his spirits as he headed for home.

His house was still devoid of light and so much colder now he knew about 'Them'. And Zac. That night he saw his parents asleep, but not asleep—they must be part of it.

As he opened the front door, he heard the floorboards creak above.

Damn, they are already up!

After stealthily moving quickly up the stairs, he took large strides across the hallway carpet, trying to cushion each landing as much as possible by over-bending his front knee. There were voices behind his parent's bedroom door, and then he saw the handle move. He stumbled the rest of the way, and squeezed through the gap in his door, before silently shutting it. He sank to his knees and let himself breathe.

The footsteps got quieter as his father headed downstairs, and he took the opportunity to scramble to his bed and pull himself into the soft embrace of the sheets. Shutting his eyes, he allowed the world to ease away.

They were on the beach — him and Ryan — looking out to the mist that was forming above the water. The humming was back with a vengeance, as was the howling wind.

"Do you feel it?" Zac asked. "Isn't it beautiful?" he said, arms outstretched and hair and t-shirt fiercely flapping around him.

The humming was louder than before, and Ryan felt it to the core. "I feel it," he responded weakly, but his words were lost in the wind.

The fog was nearly upon them when Zac began to wade into the water, "Come on in, Ry. It's so refreshing."

Waves started breaking further back. "Zac, come back — it isn't safe."

And in the distance, he could make out something approaching, something so big it monopolized the horizon. He saw it begin to curl and realized it was the biggest wave he had ever seen.

Ryan slowly started to back away, "Zac!" he screamed, and this time, he heard his words.

His friend turned around then and smiled, eyes as black as coal. "He will get you too, Ry. You can't fight him." And then he reached his hand out towards him, "Join us and bring some hell to their day."

— — —

"Morning, son!" his father's voice bellowed.

Ryan jolted upright, heart pounding, and that familiar damp feeling on his sheets.

He squinted at the light leaking through his open blinds, as both of his parents stood proudly at the end of his bed, arms folded and faces split in two with the largest grins.

"How do you feel?" his mum asked eagerly.

"Fine—fine, I guess. What time is it? You scared the hell out of me!"

"I truly hope not," his father responded and winked. "It's 9."

His mum's face changed as she walked to the edge of his bed and put a hand to his forehead, "Are you okay, son? You didn't have a nightmare, did you?"

Nobody leaves this town.

"No—no, you just woke me, that's all. I'll see you at breakfast."

"Okay, son. We have a lot to talk about, though, yes? Like how your first night was. What he had you doing, etc.—we want to hear all about it. We're so proud of you," his father said.

His parents exchanged a glance, nodded, and then made their way towards the door. Before leaving, though, his mum turned to him—her face a picture of concern, or perhaps it was suspicion. She closed the door behind her.

Oh shit. Shit. Shit!

He dressed and paced the room. There was nowhere to hide—nowhere to run. The whole town was part of this, including his best friend. *What did she mean what he had you doing? And what the fuck am I going to do?*

"Come on, son! Your mum and I are excited!" the voice boomed from downstairs.

Fuck.

"Coming!"

There was a knock at the front door then.

It would buy him time—perhaps he could sneak out the window. But he had nowhere to go.

Shit!

He'd lied before to get out of trouble, but he was going to have to come up with something special to get out of this one. Taking his time down the stairs, he had a plan—he'd seen it on CSI—open questions, turn it around. Make them spill.

They both smiled when he entered the kitchen, and his dad nudged a chair towards him.

He sat down—game face on.

"Look who's just popped round to see you, Ryan," his mum said. And from behind the fridge, Zac stepped out, "Hi, Ry!" he said.

Ryan glanced towards the door, but his father eyed him and shook his head, "All you had to do was eat one, Ryan. Now we have to do it the hard way."

"Wait. Just wait. What is going on? Why do I have to do anything? What the fuck are you talking about?"

"Language, Ryan!" his mum yelled.

"Sorry," he said, eyes to the ground. And the tears started again.

"Ryan, this has to be done," his father said with at least some empathy. "There is a price to pay for our safety; for our community. It is a beautiful place to live, but this is his land. It's a debt we have to pay."

"I don't understand!" Ryan pleaded, bawling now.

"Between the hours of midnight and six, our souls are his. We leave this place and follow the devil's beat into the darkness. And we do things. Bad things. But only to keep us all safe — to preserve our beautiful town."

"What sort of things?"

His dad looked over to his mum, "The devil's candy — it was the easy option, son. You should have taken it. We all have to do it."

"So, the old man was the devil?"

"And so was the old lady. The devil can take many forms, Ryan, but he only has so much time in the day. That's where we come in," his dad replied.

Ryan glanced at the door once more, but any thoughts of fleeing were squashed as he saw some of the other residents making their way towards the house.

"Please, Dad! Please, Mum!"

"I told you, son, we have to do this the hard way now."

Ryan looked towards his mum, but her eyes were directed towards the floor. "Mum!" Ryan begged.

His father stood up urgently, his chair skidding across the floor.

"It's going to be okay, Ry," Zac assured. "This town isn't boring, after all. You just wait and see what we can do."

The door opened then, and Robert, the bald guy from across the road, announced that it was time.

And so once again, Ryan joined a procession, but this time, heading towards the sea.

A million thoughts ran through his head as the simple task of putting one foot in front of the other became increasingly difficult. At one stage, he felt so heavy he thought he might pass out. The smell was getting stronger all the time, and the low humming quickly accelerated into an unpleasant internal pulsating. It wasn't long before the first person in the line began to replicate the humming with his mouth—a deep monotone sound that made Ryan shudder. And soon the others joined in. Locked in stride between his mother and father, he had never been so scared in his life.

As the water came into view, the bright skies once again became shrouded in cloud, and the wind began to blow his hair against his face. He felt the warmth spread down the front of his pants.

Before he knew what was happening, he was hoisted in the air by the residents. The vibration in his spine was becoming unbearable, and the dull hum beneath only served as an ominous theme to what was about to happen.

As panic set in, Ryan began to thrash violently from side to side. The motion didn't help, and the changing horizon was making him even more disoriented. He almost wished that he would pass out so he would not need to endure what was ahead.

The hotel owners, Tom and Judy, were the first in the water. And soon they were all in, relentlessly marching through the black murkiness — still humming in time to the vibration that ran down his spine. And just as the water reached the neck of Tom and Judy, they all simultaneously released him, and he fell into the cold icy blackness. Before he could even begin to try and break the surface, a dozen or so hands were on him, holding him down.

Immediately he panicked again, sucking in a mouthful of the black water — already his lungs felt as though they might explode, and he was so desperate for air. The faces above were becoming blurry as he flailed helplessly at the arms that pinned him. He even recognized his mother — the way her hair flicked up at the end. But soon, they all faded into one. The pain in his body was inconceivable — a pressure chamber of bone-crushing agony, and as he struggled, he ingested more of the water.

He felt it then, the hand on his face.

The scaly skin was harsh, and the sharp claws scratched as they brushed against his cheek. There was a sudden sharp sting as one of them pierced the flesh—he felt it sinking into him—exploring. No, not exploring, but transferring something to him—something so powerful it made his veins sing, and head spin with all the possibilities. A whisper in his head kept looping—a strange language he had never heard before—but after half a dozen times, he understood.

He turned his head towards the devil, and immediately felt an overwhelming sensation of privilege—not as though he was being punished at all—after all, this was one on one attention.

The murkiness made it difficult to see clearly, but the red eyes were unmistakable, as were the scales that extended across the creature's back. In the devil's other claw sat some of the colorful candy, and more of it glimmered seductively on the bottom of the ocean floor—like pebbles polished by the lick of the tainted tide.

Devil's candy.

The hand was removed, and the devil slinked back into the murky waters. Above Ryan was an expanse of blackness—the faces had vanished, and he felt as though he was floating—drifting through some sort of limbo. An overwhelming calmness swept over him, and suddenly, he was exhausted, eyes heavy and breathing—

He woke up gasping for breath and squinting as the light from the window shone directly into his face. He turned to look at his clock - 7 am. His immediate thought was that it was a dream, but the events that subsequently ran through his head were so vivid—the procession and the hands all over him, holding him down, and the cold touch of the black hand that he could still feel.

Besides, he felt different.

The mist, too—yes—he remembered following his father into the water and following his soul back to the house, the cloud of fog wrapped around him like a bubble.

He went down for breakfast that morning and watched some television with his proud as punch parents. Immediately, he recognized the man on the news from the beach last week— killed his family with a steak knife and tried to cut their heads off with a hedge trimmer. The television showed a picture of his wife and two children next. The mum had an arm around each of her children's shoulders. They all looked so content standing in front of the shimmering water, and with their feet planted firmly in the golden sand. The reporter said they had only just returned from an enjoyable family holiday—even gave the seaside town a mention.

"That's good for the town!" his dad said excitedly.

What the reporter didn't mention was when the police entered the premises, the victims were all lined up—the number six carved into each of their chests. The man was crying and rocking back and forth, whispering something about a kid doing it.

Ryan couldn't help but smile as he touched the scar on the side of his cheek. He tried to fight it at first, but there was something dark inside him now that yearned for more blood. He caught his dad looking at him from the other side of the couch, gushing with obvious pride, and his father returned his smile. They leaned towards each other and fist-bumped. Soon, he would go and see Zac, so they could share their stories—swap details of their deeds.

There would no longer be a fear of closing his eyes at night. He was protected. A creator now instead of a passer-by with a new story to weave each time darkness fell.

He would later learn that he was the special one—marked by the devil. Some could only infiltrate dreams and turn them into terrifying nightmares. But he could take them to a far darker place—to the gates of hell itself—and torment them into unspeakable things.

The devil said he could never leave town, and Ryan had a pretty good idea what would happen if he tried. But that was fine. He loved his home. The community was brought closer together by the secrets that bound them—such a friendly and safe place to live. And his dad said there was no such thing as a free lunch.

There is a quiet sleepy seaside town near you—idyllic, inviting, and peaceful. Your visit will stay with you long after you have returned home—if you are one of the lucky ones.

TO THE BEGINNING

by River Dixon & tara caribou

<Stream 4b>

"You know we're not supposed to go in there..." Jake's whiny little voice carried across the abandoned lot, annoying the shit out of her. "Jessie... I'll tell dad... I will!" God. Little brothers. She loved him, but he was also the biggest scaredy-cat she knew. "I just want to check it out a little... stay here if you want... I'm going in."

There were rumors that surrounded the place. No one was allowed here. No one. Even the grown-ups stayed away. But Jess had got bored this summer. She wasn't afraid, no matter what they all said. The walkway going up to the long-abandoned estate was pitted, missing bricks, with weeds growing in the cracks. The lawns on either side had long overgrown and then burned away in the summer suns of years past. Behind the multi-towered home lay the forest of local legend. That's where she ultimately wanted to go. In the back of her mind, she could hear their father's voice, warning them, yet the pull of the unknown was even stronger.

Standing on the porch, she took a deep breath, felt the boards beneath her feet flex as she shifted her weight from foot to foot. She slid a hand into the pocket of her jeans and felt the compass her grandfather had given her. He once told her that it didn't matter what direction she chose, only that she knows which direction she's going. That hadn't made any sense to her at the time. Still doesn't. But grandpa was always kind of different. Her dad would say that grandpa had still waters which run deep. She didn't understand that one either. She loved listening to his stories about all the wild adventures he had gone on throughout his life. Her favorite being how he met her grandmother at a street market in Morocco and saved her from marauding invaders, even though grandma insisted they had met during the war.

Grandpa had told her everyone was wrong about this place, the house and the forest beyond. He said that people simply did not understand and when people don't understand something, they tend to fear it. As a matter of fact, they had planned to explore the area together, but grandpa had died before they ever got the chance. Now, it's her turn to be the adventurer. She would walk right into this old house and prove to everyone there's nothing to be afraid of.

"Jessie, come ba-" Her little brother's voice came to an abrupt silence. As Jessie turned there was a blinding flash of soft white light, then snow-like particles filled the air around her. Her chest gasped and heaved as she tried to regain the breath which had been knocked out of her. There was no sound . . . No feeling... A cold numbness, weightlessness.

<insert Stream 11c>

State Destination. Her eyes flickered. She heard a soft hum around her. The air smelled slightly of ozone. A whir and a click. *Please State Destination.* The gentle female voice seemed to come from all around her. She blinked open her eyes and the light faded some but not entirely. She stood in a bright stark white room, which seemed to provide its own internal glow with no lighting to speak of.

It did bear some resemblance to the foyer she'd just stepped through, same size and shape, entrance and exits… except this room had no old artwork on the walls or furniture. In fact, as she looked about her, she realized she wasn't even standing on a floor. She was floating right inside the doorway, weightless. There were panels on the walls with images and lettering and what looked to be small maps, but none like she'd seen in school. Above the archway that led deeper into the house there hung a sign which read Travelers Must Sign In, with an arrow pointing through. Below that in a smaller script, it read: Compass Keepers Pass Through with a tree silhouette engraved on either side of the lettering.

Do you need assistance? Her grandpa's worn compass felt heavy in her pocket and cool to the touch. She looked at the map before her. An inner knowledge and recognition stirred within her breast. "It doesn't matter what direction you choose…" his words echoed in her ear. Her hand stretched forth.

— — —

<Stream 24m>

"Jess."

An unrecognizable force began to shake her body.

"Jess… JESS!... wake up!"

She felt the grip of hands on her shoulders. Eyes open, the room came in as she focused on David's face. Drenched in sweat, the thin white sheet twisted and bunched around her legs.

"Baby, are you okay?"

"I think so, yeah, I'm okay. The umm- I was having that dream again. My brother…"

"I know, I heard you calling out his name. Was it the same dream?"

"Yeah… SHIT! What time is it?"

"It's six-twenty."

"Oh, good, I've got time."

"When's your appointment?"

"Nine, but I am supposed to be there at eight forty-five."

"I wish I could go with you, but I can't miss work today. This is pretty much my last chance to keep this account… and my job."

"I understand, it's fine. I can handle this. I'm finally getting help, and that's what's important. This is a new beginning. I'm going to figure this out."

--- --- ---

Jess approached the window behind which sat a neatly groomed woman tapping quickly across her keyboard. She cleared her throat, "I'm here for a nine o'clock appointment with Dr. Tillyou."

"Just a sec," the woman tapped out across a few screens on her computer before handing across a clipboard which held several colored sheets of paper. "Here, review your personal information and insurance information for accuracy please."

She scanned the document, "yeah, everything looks correct."

"Great, have a seat right over there, and the nurse will be with you shortly."

"The nurse?"

"Yes. The nurse will take you back first to get your vitals and then the doctor will see you."

"Oh, okay, thanks."

Jess sat on a padded bench next to an enormous, fake potted plant. There were a couple of magazines on the table in front of her but nothing she was interested in reading. The walls looked old, a sickly dirty yellow and the ceiling tiles above her head were covered in water stains. She picked up a pamphlet about suicide prevention then another about the opioid epidemic. A speaker hung crooked on the wall behind her, producing nothing but static. *My God,* she thought, *if people aren't crazy enough when they get here, that damn static will push them over the edge.* She considered asking the receptionist to tune the radio to a station actually playing some music, but before she could, a door opened, and a woman with a clipboard stepped through.

"Jessica... Jessica D-"

The static behind her grew in intensity suddenly overpowering every other sense in her body. She saw the woman's face turn to concern, mouthing words she couldn't hear. *So loud. So damn loud.* Jess put her hands to her head trying to muffle out the sound but instead felt herself floating forward and then her view went sideways as she fell to the dirty tiles. Numb, she felt nothing. Everything began to grey at the edges while the static continued to grow deafening. And as her vision completely faded, she heard a man's voice, "I thought it'd never take..."

— — —

<Stream 4b>

"Stay here then, you're just a little baby!"

"I ain't a baby Jessie, don't say it. I'm not a-scared."

"Yes, you are, you're a stupid little baby, and you can just stay here." With hate in her eyes, Jessie pushed her little brother to the ground, turned her back to him and walked toward the house. With or without him, she was going to see what all the fuss was about.

— — —

<Perception 9r>

Lights passing overhead. A too-bright hallway. Doors. Faint forms on either side of her.

"She's awake."

Pinch on the forearm. Heat in a vein. Darkness.

"Jessica."

Snapping. *Fingers snapping?*

"Jessica…. the procedure went well. You'll be groggy for a day or so, but you did really well. We got so much information that we needed. Go home. Sleep it off."

— — —

"Where was she this time?"

"She was with her 'husband' and played through the psychiatrist scenario."

"Oh, yes, she is quite fond of that one," they both chuckled softly.

The two white-clad figures stood over an unconscious young girl, her wrists and ankles tied securely to the bed rails. The walls of the room covered with crude drawings of two figures, one taller than the other and each with a compass rose sketched in the corner. The girl began to struggle against her restraints, moaning. Eyes starting to rapidly flutter beneath the lids. The man handed his clipboard to the woman, who took out a pen and started writing.

— — —

<Fragment 16t>

"JAKE!!!!" Jessie screamed from where she stood at the tree line. "JAKE, WHERE ARE YOU JAKE???"

She scanned back and forth, listening for any sound of movement. Nothing. Her heart was pounding out of her chest, she couldn't catch her breath. "JAKE!!!"

I've got to find him.

She swallowed hard against the lump in her throat, put her head down and stepped between two trees. A large fern brushed against her thigh, the mossy ground absorbing each step. It was silent in there as her mind raced. She removed the compass from her pocket and held it in front of her. Which way would he go?

Before her lay an overgrown trail, barely discernible. Glancing at the compass, it pointed the way clearly without the trepidation she felt within her breast. *He's been missing too long. Far too long.*

Time yawned. She continued on, sometimes taking a branching trail, sometimes passing them by. The compass continued guiding the way unwaveringly. She'd learned to trust it, the many times she had walked these paths. She lost count by now, but it'd never let her down. A rustle just ahead.

"Jake?!" A quiet moan. Her pace increased. "Jake??" Through a thick patch and there he lay. At least, she thought it was him. Kneeling next to the crumpled form, she gently turned him over, "oohhh Jake…. I told you to stay put…"

There beside her lay no longer a young boy, but instead a thin, worn teenager. It was definitely him though; but not from this time, she intuited. His threadbare clothes clung to his far-too-thin frame. His skin was tanned and covered in scars that reminded her of those left by octopus suckers she'd seen in one of grandpa's books. "Damn it, Jake," she whispered.

— — —

<Stream 11c>

Upon reaching the wall, Jess stretched forth her palm, gently touching the images and words found there. The hair on her arms suddenly rose as she read the words like a journal entry written there, "Jessica always did prove herself stronger than her younger sibling Jake. Time and again she rose to each challenge set before her. No matter what we threw at her, she met each head-on with steely determination and grit. She proved far greater a threat than an asset, in the end, so we collectively had decided, and in response, the Vault was designed and built just for one such as her." Suddenly the compass felt very, very heavy in her pocket.

— — —

<Fragment 21t>

"Here, eat this." An outstretched hand offered Jess one of the last remaining rations.

"I'm not hungry. Leave me alone," Jess hissed.

The bunker was dark; cold but familiar. She hated being back here. Always waiting. She didn't have time for this.

"So, are we going to talk or are you just going to ignore me again?"

"I have nothing to say to you," Jess barked.

"You know, our time together is limited, I can't help you if you don't let me in. Jessica, look at me–"

Jess turned to the figure with a look of disgust and retaliation in her eyes. "You were never here to help me. Don't say that to me. You put me in this place, locked me away, filled me full of your poison and watched me like a lab animal. You really want to help me?? Then let me go back."

"Back where? There's nowhere left to go. You are well aware of that, *you're* the one who showed *me*."

"Don't play your fucking games with me!!" Jess screamed. "You know what I can do to you… And I'll do it again. Stop fucking with my head!"

"Okay, there's no need to get yourself so upset. You know you have the lead in all this. Tell me, where do you want to go?"

Jess stood up. "To the beginning."

− − −

<Perception 9r>

"No... I'm not part of this, I'm not your experiment," Jess sobbed.

"No? Then what are you? Why are you here?"

"I... I'm just-"

"You're just what? Here by mistake? I know that line of thinking can make things easier for some, but I assure you, my child, there are no mistakes here. Either accept that or don't, it doesn't matter to us. But we have limited time, and we must get started."

"Please, I have to go, I have to find him," Jess pleaded.

"Yes, this is most interesting. Where is it you would like to go?"

Jess turned to the figure with tears in her eyes. "To the beginning."

− − −

The man in the white lab coat stood before a small board of peers. A clipboard holding a sheaf of papers trembled in his hands. There was a palpable concern in the air. "She's fractured."

Murmurs erupt. "Shit." "How...?" "You said it wouldn't happen again."

His head hung a little, shoulders slumped in defeat. "I know. I know. Believe me…. she's so much more than we expected. More than we were prepared for, really." His fingers pinched the bridge of his nose. "Listen. We have an idea. It's… risky… but given the circumstances…."

"Let's hear it." One of them spoke with irritated authority.

"We want to bring her in. But she's got to do it on her own. There's no other way."

More protests. A minor argument. In the end, they all knew he was right. She had to be stopped. She was rewriting the histories as she walked the paths. All their times were short.

— — —

<Stream 11c>

There was only one path in which she could *remember*. It was on this one in which she found herself once again. If she sat and really thought about it, she'd be able to remember all the other paths. Remember when the world hadn't gone to shit yet, and the Titans hadn't taken over. Remember when Jake was still her little brother tagging along where he wasn't wanted; when Grandpa told stories that had a ring of truth but little understanding; when life was simple. But then she also remembered David and his strong arms at night; or a stark white room with maps and directions; and then there was the terror of the straps around her wrists and ankles…. oh, she could remember it all…. when her dreams became reality. But then, she learned to control those dreams. Monsters and fears and childish misunderstandings, made real and flesh. Of course, by then it was too late. They couldn't control her. Jess knew she needed someone to reign her in, though. Knew it with every fiber of her being. She just needed to get back to the beginning.

Knowledge flowed through her veins, and she felt the now-familiar blinding flash of light and temporary mind disorientation. With purpose, she quickly moved through the room. *State Destination*. Without consulting her compass this time, she answered briskly, "here," and lightly tapped one of the maps. "Back here."

— — —

<Stream 9a>

Her father was no carpenter, but he had done the best he could. Made of mostly scrap wood and parts salvaged from the dump, the treehouse was the most amazing thing Jessie had ever seen. This was her place. Well, Jake's too, but as the older sister, she was in charge. She would often climb up first and make Jake stand at the bottom, trying to guess whatever password she had come up with that day. The woods behind their family home could be a scary place at times but full of all the adventure her mind could come up with. The treehouse offered protection from all the bandits, witches, orcs and goblins. Even the evil queen could not touch them there.

Jake played in the corner with his action figures, and Jessie intensely studied a crude map she had drawn depicting a section of forest; the section where the Dagger of Wellspring is believed to be hidden. That would be their next adventure for sure. She grabbed the old military backpack her grandfather had given her and began packing the necessities for their quest. She turned to Jake.

"You better start getting your bag ready. We're leaving soon."

Jake continued to play with his toys, offering no response or acknowledgment.

"Jake! Did you hear me? Start getting your stuff ready!"

Jake seemed as though he didn't hear her.

"JAKE!! Listen to me!" Jessie yelled, frustrated with her little brother. Her eye caught a rusty nail sticking out from a board in the floor, a calm voice spoke-

"Going out on adventures like that can be fun, what sort of items did you pack in your bag?"

Jessie stared at the nail, wondering where the hammer was. She needed to fix that before somebody caught their foot on it.

<extract Perception 9r>

"You two had a lot of good times in that treehouse, didn't you?" The voice took the form of a man in a white coat. "Remembering the good memories, every tiny detail of the moment, the sights, sounds, smells, is something that will help bring you to where we need to be."

Jessica turned her face to the man with a look of confusion, the nail and the treehouse and Jake fading away, "Dr. Tillyou?"

"Yes... Oh, good. We went deep that time. Excellent. *Excellent.*" His pen briskly scratched on the clipboard.

"What are you talking about?"

"I think that is enough for today. You did well. I'll let the nurse know we're finished. She'll bring you some juice and help you to the bathroom." The man rose from his chair, looked up at a camera mounted on the ceiling and nodded. Prompted by the sound of a buzzer, he opened the door, and walked out.

The young girl, dressed in a loose white gown and strapped to the bed, struggled against her restraints. The realization, the memory of where she was, set in, and she began to scream.

— — —

<Stream 24m>

The first time Jessie altered time, she wasn't initially aware she'd done so. She and David had been madly in love and decided to spend two weeks in Hawaii, hiking and bumming around. On the sixth day, he had asked her to marry him, on the eighth he was dead... and then he wasn't. They'd been hiking up a little higher than they should've been. Closer to the edge than they should have been. One rolled ankle and over he went. She watched his body hit a ledge and continue on. She screamed and sobbed as she raced back down. Beginning within her palms, Jessie felt a glowing deep inside, and she knew he would be alright. As she approached him, his body twisted and bruised, she pictured there in her mind David as she knew him: her lover and now fiancé. Whole and beautiful. Wiping the tears from her cheeks, she knelt at his side. The wind lifted, and it was almost as if there was snow falling around her. She felt the shift and when she opened her eyes all was the same except there! his chest rose and fell. He remembered the long fall, his body crunching to the ground and the miracle that he was still in fact alive. Together they decided it was destiny and it was a sign they were meant to be one. Looking back, Jessie realized that was the first time she'd changed a path.

Then she began changing more. Intentionally and with purpose. Always for good in the beginning and yet she hadn't fully understood that changing one path altered others in ways you didn't realize until it was much too late. There were consequences. You couldn't go back, only sideways. She slipped along one path, following the guiding compass and found herself back on the line where Titans had devoured most of world. Shit. Talking about Titans on most paths would land you in the crazy house. But on this one, they were real and powerful. Yet for reasons unknown, they ignored her presence. Did they not see her or was she something altogether different? All she knew was, it was, at this stage, one of the safest places she could rest.

— — —

"Doctor! Quick! She's going deep again!"

"Holy shit! Quick Quick! Get the Ambuzel!"

"....Doctor? You remember what happened last time we tried using that on h— "

"I know, damn it! I know! We've got to stop her."

The shackled girl pulled and strained, eyes flying open as she let out an ear-piercing shriek. "The beginning!"

— — —

<Stream 24m>

She looked at David, his eyes had a sparkle to them, as they always did first thing in the morning. He was smiling.

"You're here," he said lovingly.

Jess's head was clouded, confused by his statement. *Is it really that simple?*

"Yeah, I'm here." Jess rolled to her side and pulled the sheet over her head.

David put a gentle hand on her shoulder. "Hey baby, what's wrong? Is it that dream again? Your bro-"

Jess shot up in the bed, pushed David away from her and screamed. "Why do you always ask me that? The *dream*, my *brother*, that's all you ever fucking say to me!"

"I'm sorry, Jess, I don't understand. Why are you acting like this?"

<note fragmentation>

Jess got out of bed, walked to the mirror and stared at the dirty, tattered white gown which loosely draped her thin body. She turned to David. "Who are you?"

"Jess, what do you mean?"

She turned and walked to David's side of the bed, grabbed him by the back of the hair and pulled his face close to hers. She glared in his eyes; they still sparkled.

"I said, who-the-fuck-are-you?" Jess demanded through clenched teeth.

"I don't know how to answer that." David appeared strangely calm.

"Who are you?" Jess repeated.

David reached back and released his hair from her grasp. "You tell me who I am. Yours is the voice, Jess."

Jess shook her head, "this isn't right, I'm fucking losing it . . . I need to see Dr. Tillyou . . ."

<insert Perception 9r>

"Then see him," David stated. "You can do anything you want. I can offer only a momentary reprieve, respite in a time of need. Do you hear the voice? It's you. Yours is the voice that's been calling you back home."

"You're fucking crazy," Jess stepped back from David. "Stop messing with my head…"

"Here, feel this," David took Jess's hand in his. "Is this not real? Do you not feel me?"

Jess felt his hand squeeze hers, and she started to shake.

"I don't know anymore," her voice quivered.

"Yes, you do. And you are the only one who does know. You had better go see Dr. Tillyou now. It's getting late."

— — —

"I'm glad you're here. Come in, sit down."

The old man took off his hat and shook his head, "I don't want to sit, I want to know what's going on."

The man in the white coat, sitting behind the desk took off his glasses and rubbed his temple. "It's complicated. I'll tell you what I know so far, but there's a lot we don't understand yet. Here, please, have a seat," he gestured with his hand, vaguely indicating the chair facing him.

The old man sat. "I just don't understand, she's been here for over a year, and it seems like she's just getting worse every day."

"We're trying every option available to us. Shock, pharmaceuticals, induced coma, restraints, cold treatment, guided meditations, and more therapy sessions than I can count. Your granddaughter is... resilient and consistently resists all forms of treatment. Some days she expresses a desire to come to terms with reality. Other days she absolutely refuses." His fingers tapped a stack of thick files resting on his desk. "We are rapidly running out of legal options here. She's slipping deeper and deeper away as she loses sight of real life." A pause and a sigh, "now, I'm just going to put this forward… we've heard talk of a highly experimental procedure that, while dangerous and frankly illegal in this country, is generating excellent results in patients with similar issues."

Tears shone in the elderly man's eyes as he whispered, "tell me."

— — —

<Stream 9a>

"Jake? Are you listening to me? Get ready. I want an early start if we're going to find the Lost Dagger of Wellspring. I know we can find it."

"Okay! Okay, Jessie! Hold on!" Jake set something in the corner of the treehouse and began shoving random items into his backpack.

"Come on! Wait? Why are you putting crayons in there? That's dumb. We don't need crayons where we're going… actually, keep them. We might be able to trade them to the witch at the Big Stump for something good. Have you seen grandpa's compass? It's not in its spot…."

Looking worried, Jake's cheeks flushed, "Jessie! Don't be mad!"

"What have you done, Jake??"

— — —

Standing before a bank of screens, the two figures in their white coats stood transfixed watching as the young girl in 27c underwent their latest experiment. "How'd you get his permission?"

A grim chuckle. "How I always do: I lied. Told him that it had been done before in other countries."

"That always seems to reel 'em in."

"It's all psychology. Tell them it's dangerous. It's forbidden. But gets results.... let's just pray that this time, it really does."

"And if it doesn't-"

Turning to his comrade, "if it doesn't, I fear nothing will."

— — —

<Fragment 16t transmuting fragmentation>

Sitting on the trail, holding her brother in her arms, gashes, and marks marring his flesh, Jessie felt very little hope for him. He just had to pull through. Had to. He let out a groan. "....Jake? I'm here, you big baby." She spoke through tears, forced bravado. *Dad told her to protect him. But she hadn't had she? Wait. Dad. How long had it been? This wasn't right. This wasn't how Jake di-.*

Everything faded to grey then white. Particles like snow floating around her. She looked about herself and recognized the foyer. The mansion. The memory of where she'd been quickly fading until she couldn't even remember its echo. A panic began to rise in her throat. She tried conjuring up any memory at all, but it was like water in a sieve.

"Help me! Somebody! Grandpa!! Help!"

Do you need assistance?

"Yes! Yes! Where am I?? I need my grandpa. Where's Jake? My dad?"

Please wait as I access that information... Processing....

A doctor has been summoned. Please remain calm.

— — —

"Doctor. It appears the first round of treatment may have actually had a positive impact. She safely left the reality and came back to the clinic."

"Good. Good." He consulted his clipboard of notes before continuing, jotted a swift note. "Keep observing and administer the next treatment just as soon as you see she's in another delusion."

"Yes, Doctor.... will she be okay?"

"Only time will tell."

— — —

Looking at the bank of screens and then down at the sheaf of notes and back to the screens, the old man narrowed his eyes and screwed up his face, clearly trying to make sense of what he saw there. "How does it-?"

"How does it all work?" The woman responded quickly, softly. PR work was reading the customer and responding before they even knew they had a question to ask. She smiled gently at him.

Holding out a bundle of wires, each connected into a single device at one end and the other end a long extremely thin needle. It looked terrifying even to her. Tapping a needle with a carefully manicured nail she explained. "We insert each needle electrode into key parts of your granddaughter's brain. I assure you, it is painless and will not harm her." Holding a few separate, "these three green wires here deliver special electrical pulses in different wavelengths and amperages." Then switching to the rest, "the remaining four have the ability to read the images that are occurring within her mind at any given time. The images are fed into a computer which in turn displays on these screens." Her hand fluttered toward the wall. "In this way, we are able to, in essence, watch her dreams and also guide them using the electric pulses combined with our trained psychologists, who speak directly to her."

His voice trembled slightly as he asked, "and that white wire there?"

"Oh, this? Yes, this is a special wire. It's the one that will help snap your granddaughter out of each fantasy as she lives it. Think of it as eating away all those bad thoughts. Until finally, we'll be left with just reality. Then she'll be able to heal and move on." Her saccharine smile didn't help his stomach much. But his love for his granddaughter was even greater.

"You said it's possible to speak to her while she's under, can umm… Can I speak to her?"

The woman glanced uncomfortably at the viewing window. "That's not for me to say. You would need to speak with the doctor regarding that. Oh, here he comes now."

The door swung open, and the doctor approached the old man.

"And what would you say to her?" The doctor questioned.

"I don't know. I just want to talk to her, tell her it's okay. Let her know we don't blame her for what happened, we just want her back."

The doctor shook his head, "no, no, that would make no difference. She wouldn't even know what you were talking about. You have to understand; she has buried the memory of that day deeper than we have ever experienced before. And we have to be cautious in our methods to bring her back. We have no idea how she will respond once that memory returns to the surface."

"But I have to do something," the old man insisted. "She's so alone, so hurt, I can't just leave her here like this, day after day. I have to do something."

The doctor looked to the woman, and she nodded. "There is something we could try. There is the ability to force her back to that day. We hadn't considered it an option before because like I said, we don't know what will happen. But we can perform the procedure on you at the same time and insert you into her experience. You can be there when it happens and talk her through it. Do you think that is something you would be able to do?"

"I will do anything for her. Anything."

"Of course, there are a number of risks for both you and her, but I get the impression you are not overly concerned with that. I will need you to sign some papers though. Liability waiver, consent, things of that nature. Do you want some time to think about this or should we get started?"

"I don't need to think about it, just tell me what you need me to do."

"When we start the procedure, I will need to gather some baseline data. To do this, we will first need to inject you into a positive experience from your past. Ideally, one where you experienced a wide range of emotions. Do you have anything in mind?"

"Yes. I know exactly the memory."

"Alright then, let's get started."

— — —

<implantation, memory coding>

Fear gripped the young soldier as he was carried on a stretcher into the makeshift medical facility. Shouts and dim, flickering lights filled the room. Two medics lifted him onto a cot and then hurried back out to the truck that contained the others. He couldn't feel his left arm, and the pain in his head was unbearable. His abdomen too. He called out for help, but no one seemed to hear.

"Please, somebody... Help me. Please."

His thoughts went to his mother. The last afternoon before he left; sitting on the porch, drinking lemonade. He could tell she wanted to cry but was trying to be strong. She knew what war was capable of taking away. His uncle, her little brother, had already died over there. He tried his best to reassure her that everything would be fine. He promised the war would be over soon, and he would be back home before she knew it. The truth was, he was more terrified than he's ever been; of anything, but he was determined not to show it. He didn't want her to worry, although he knew she would regardless. And now, he feared he may never see her again; that he won't be able to keep his promise.

"Somebody... Anybody. Can you hear me? I don't want to die."

A hand fell tenderly across his forehead.

"Who said anything about dying?" the woman's voice was soft but strong.

"I don't want to die here. Please, don't let me die here. It's so far from home." He stared through the dizzying double-vision as best he could. The ringing in his ears tried to drown out her voice.

"And where is home, soldier?" She was dressed in white. The small cap adorned with a red cross tilted slightly on top of her head.

"Kansas."

"Oh, my, you *are* a long way from home. Tell me something, what do you like to do back there in Kansas?"

"I, ahh," she patted his forehead with a damp, cool rag, "spend uh- most of my time on our family farm."

"That sounds nice," she smiled. "My family has a farm too, in Illinois. I miss the quiet. The calmness of the midwestern evenings. Sitting on the porch with my dog, Ben, while my father smoked his cigar."

"I have a dog…" his voice trailed off as the pain overtook him. He looked into her eyes and she took his hand. She was the last thing he saw before passing out, and the first thing when he awoke after surgery.

"She's quite beautiful," a woman's voice echoed. "Such a rich memory, thank you for sharing it with us. That gave us everything we needed; we're ready now."

— — —

<insertion Perception 9r, disengaged mode>

The old man was surrounded by trees. His granddaughter is on her knees, screaming and shaking his grandson.

"Jake!! Get up! Jake... Please, Jake..."

The old man put a hand on her shoulder, "Jess-"

"Grandpa, you're here... What are you...? They got him! I tried to protect him, I'm so sorry... They got him..."

The old man got down on his knees and grabbed Jess by the shoulders, "Honey, what are you talking about? Who got him?"

She was shaking uncontrollably. "He's hurt. Hurt real bad. He's not moving. They got him..."

"Jess, look at me girl, who are you talking about?"

"The orcs... The witch, they got Jake. They hurt him. We gotta get outta here, they'll come back... They'll get us too. We have to get out of here, we have to hide... RUN!"

Jess broke free of the old man's grasp and disappeared into the trees. He called out after her, and a woman's voice answered. *"You're doing fine. Now, we're going back to forty-five seconds before the incident. We need you to only observe, do not attempt to intervene. I repeat, do not intervene. Once you have witnessed what happened, we will bring you back here, just prior to her running away. Do you understand?"*

"Yes, I understand." The old man reached his hand toward the lifeless body of his grandson.

— — —

Jake clutched his backpack with both hands and began to cry. "I'm sorry Jessie, I'm sorry. It was an accident."

The old man took a step back and crouched in the corner of the treehouse.

"It's alright," the woman's voice echoed in his head. "They can't see you."

Jessie followed Jake's eyes to where he looked in the corner of the treehouse. She saw the edge of her precious compass. She went to it and lifted it up. It fell apart in her hand, pieces dropping to the wooden floor, rolling out between the cracks in the planks and falling to the ground below. Her face turned red. "JAKE!!!" she screeched before turning on him. The young boy clutched his bag tightly to his chest and backed away from his sister; sobbing turned to wailing.

His heel caught on a nail which stuck up a bit through the floor. His eyes went wide as he lost his balance and he began to fall, almost in slow motion. Both the boy and his bag tumbling backward, slipping through the open door and down, down, down to the grass below.

The old man cried out. Jessie did the same. She crossed to the edge and looked down on the still, silent form of her brother, his neck at an unnatural angle across the tree's roots.

The scene shifted again and there she was, kneeling beside Jake, touching his face. Prodding him. Attempting to wake him. The old man could see the realization as it set in.

"Jake!! Get up! Jake... Please, Jake..."

The old man put a hand on her shoulder, "Jess-"

"Grandpa, you're here... What are you...? They got him! I tried to protect him, I'm so sorry... They got him..."

He pulled the young girl into his arms tightly. "Jessie, my girl. It was an accident. Just an accident. I love you, please don't leave me too."

She was shaking uncontrollably. "He's hurt. Hurt real bad. He's not moving. They got him... The orcs... The witch, they got Jake. They hurt him. We gotta get outta here, they'll come back... They'll get us too. We have to get out of here, we have to hide... RUN!"

Jessie tried to pull away, but the old man was ready for it. "No Jessie. He's dead. Jake is dead, but it was just an accident. It's not your fault. Please believe me!" Tears poured from his eyes. The thought of her living in her delusions for the rest of her life scared him. First, he lost his grandson. Then his own son to grief and despair and now his granddaughter. He couldn't bear it. "Please Jessie... don't go away..."

— — —

The girl stilled in her restraints. Opened her eyes. "Grandpa?" she called.

"Tell us about your grandpa," Doctor Tillyou intoned. He pressed a button on his pad.

She felt a slight tinge behind her ear. "Grandpa gave me my compass and told me that it didn't matter what direction I chose, only that I know which direction I'm going…. do you know what that means, Doctor?"

"It means you're doing very well, Jessie. Very well. Now, tell me about the Titans, and how you brought them here…"

— — —

Conclusions: the patient in room 27c known as "Jessie" continues to provide excellent results now that we have learned to manipulate her mental abilities in a controlled and safe way. Connecting her at times with the self-administered patient in 52b, known to her as "Grandpa" has markedly improved her abilities and resilience. The old man himself seems quite content and docile to remain in such a condition so long as we keep her within his own delusions. The Vault continues on with its forward-thinking and revolutionary leaps in time manipulation and population control.

THE CAT

by Mark Ryan

"I am not crazy; my reality is just different from yours."
The Cheshire cat, Alice in wonderland

VISITOR

Nothing in the world wailed and screamed like little Sally Reeves, the girl who lived at number 5 Birch Lane. She heard her now even before seeing the child as she walked down the road leading back to her cottage. That hollering, that wailing. It seemed all she ever did was cause a ruckus. Mrs. Macready had lived through the London Blitz, bombs falling night after night with cries and noise filling the skies. And yet the sound that seemed to come from Sally Reeves topped it all.

Mrs. Macready made her way back from the little shop in the village. The shop was small and local, doubling up as the region's post office; a family-run affair where you could buy their homemade jam at the counter while getting your stamps. She hadn't needed much, a few bits and pieces. Robert from *Help the Aged* took them once a week to the big out-of-town supermarket to get their groceries. She and Joyce from across the road would sit together in the minibus and chat nonstop there and back, giggling like schoolgirls.

But this Sunday morning she had needed some extra milk and a loaf of bread, so she had trudged down the small hilly road of Angleton to the local shop. The post office was naturally closed, it being the Lord's day, but she had filled her basket with extras that she hadn't gone in for while she chatted to Agnes, who had urged her to pick up a jar of jam, freshly made; that season's plum.

She trudged now, back up the hill with her little wicker basket groaning at the weight of the unintended purchases, against Mrs. Macready's seventy-two-year-old arms. And the noise! That wailing child. Lord knows what she had to complain about all the time. She would hear her screaming in the garden, shouting and cursing at her older brother. Her screams were the shrill kind that would cut through your bones like a ghost through your skull.

Mrs. Macready was a kindly old woman. Usually pleasant around children and known to the mothers in the village as someone who the kids liked, despite having none of her own. But Sally Reeves caused her many a time to mutter 'the little shit' under her breath when she heard the noise the girl always seemed to be making.

She hurried past their cottage, their monstrous 4X4 sticking out of the drive onto the pathway, causing her to step out into the road to get past. Their sleepy village had little traffic, yet a black car came hurtling down the road towards her, hastening her return to pathway and into the safety of her own home.

The Gables was a small and picturesque cottage that sat at the top of the small hill in the village. Its little thatched roof and quaint English garden, which was the result of a lot of toil and hard work on her account, was the quintessential English cottage. Her back garden stretched off for miles, where apple orchards and vegetable rows grew in their own private ecstasy. It made way for the rolling hills of Standthorpe Valley, which undulated like a huge green sea as far as the eye could strain. A view consumed many a time daily by Mrs. Macready who would stare from her windows down into the valley below, content with her little slice of heaven.

She made it inside quickly, eager for a cup of tea and slice of toast to spread the much talked of plum jam upon. After the items were all put away and the tea was brewing, she nipped out to the recycling bin to get rid of the empty boxes. These bins she tucked away around the side of the house, keeping the aesthetics of her little cottage complete from the front and those passers-by who would silently compliment her. At least that is what she thought.

She heard the sounds of the Sally child rolling over the hedge as she stepped out the front door, she shook her head and light-footed it across her neatly trimmed lawn when she stopped suddenly. There on her wall, a large ginger cat stood upright and staring at her.

Mrs. Macready was a lover of animals; most old people are; but cats had never been ones that she'd fussed over. She was more of a dog person, having kept spaniels most of her life. But this cat was unusual, she could see that right away. Its intense eyes seem to lock onto her.

"Hullo," she said aloud to the cat, wondering if that might make it dart off in fright. The cat continued to stare at her, curiously. She watched it for a few more moments before shaking her head and carrying on around the side of the cottage to the recycling bin. She turned around to look at her wall, and the cat had disappeared. She thought her movements must had scared it off, most cats stare at you wide-eyed for a second before hurtling away. She was unsure whose animal it was, no one she knew around here had a cat, and there weren't any new people in the village as far as she knew. 'Oh well,' she thought to herself and walked back around to the front door.

On her welcome mat stood the cat, its ginger hair glistening in the Sunday morning sunshine.

"Oh you, what are you playing at?" she said, casting glances around for fear of either the owners secretly watching her, or more furry visitors.

The cat meowed and shook its small little body.

"Well you're not coming in, so don't even think about it," she said, and breached her own doorstep then began to open and close her door quickly. The cat slipped in, which she had a feeling it might.

"Oi, what...come here," she said, leaving the door open and going after the little beast.

She followed it into her living room, a small nook of a thing at the front of the cottage. The low beams were fine for her and even the cat, but for anyone else over five foot, the room became an annoyance for their neck, and a pain on the skull. She had the room as she liked it, which happened to fit the mold of country comfort. A little log fire, not currently blazing, and two small floral armchairs facing one another were all that could really fit into the little cubby. She and her husband used to sit in the chairs, the log fire burning away merrily, catching their eyes in the dancing flames as they read their own books or newspapers; glancing up occasionally to watch the other. A picture of her late husband had pride of place on the mantel above the fire, his cheeky smile grinning out into the room, reminding her of the times they had and that have passed.

That cat had jumped up into his chair, circling a spot a few times before coming to rest its bottom down and stare at her, almost tauntingly.

"What are you doing there, come on; I've had enough of you playing, silly bugger," she said coming into the room, swooping her arms in an attempt to move the cat.

It remained sitting, staring at her.

She stood on the rug by the fire looking at this creature who was now glancing back and forth between herself and the picture of her husband on the mantel.

"Come on, shoo." She said, carefully flicking the cat down off the chair. The cat leapt and returned to its spot where it had sat, defiant to her shooing and flicking. She did this a few times before giving up.

"Just like him, you are: stubborn," she said, casting her hand towards the picture. "He was ginger too, until it all began to fall out. Blamed me for that of course, stress. Stress, what did he have to be stressed about I ask you?!" She sighed and turned from the cat and its territorial stance. "Well, I'm making my tea so sit there if you must. But you're not staying long." And with that she left the room and went back to the kitchen to finish making her tea and toast, closing the front door on her way.

To her surprise, the cat followed her, and was soon prowling the kitchen; sniffing at things and jumping up on the worktop.

She watched as it moved about the room, curiously sniffing at wooden spoons and flicking its tail against the cupboard doors.

"Bet you'll be wanting something to eat or drink now?" she said, the cat, seeming to hear her, looked up expectantly.

"Arthur, I'll call you, just like my husband. He was always looking for something to drink. Always coming in when I was busy, making a fuss. Come on then, down from there and I'll get you some milk."

She went to her fridge and took out the milk bottle and poured some into a small saucer she got from her cupboard. She smiled as the cat lapped up the milk, seemingly hungry after all its exploration of the kitchen.

"Thirsty, I see," she said. The cat purred in appreciation.

She drank her own tea and finished her toast. The jam wasn't as nice as last year's offerings, the plums not as sweet as they could be, in her opinion. She cleaned up the cup and plates and thought it best to send Arthur outside now before he got too comfortable. A part of herself mindful of having named him already, the attachment perhaps fusing in the small time together. She picked him up and made her way to the door. He purred at her, and she looked into his eyes; seeing flashes there of something else. She opened the door and plopped him down onto the mat.

"That's your lot for today, now go and do what cats do," she said and bid farewell to her unexpected guest, shutting the door and disappearing inside to do what old people do.

RETURN

She woke early, as was her custom. She could hear the wind outside blowing harshly against the thin windows of her cottage. She lay there listening to the rain and the scratching of the branches against the walls. But along with this scratching, came another sound.

Down the stairs she went, tying her dressing gown as she descended. She knew exactly what to expect as she opened the front door, heaving the huge latch open.

"I knew you having a taste of the good life would be a slippery slope," she said to the cat, who darted inside as soon as the door came open. It shook itself once inside, its ginger fur fuzzing up as the rain water was expelled. Its caterwauling now ceased.

"Well, don't be getting too comfortable today. This isn't a halfway house. Soon as the rain stops, you'll be out," she said, yet she went into the front room to start the fire, making things cozy. After this she made her way into the kitchen and begin to prepare some milk and food for the cat, her heart already making room for it now.

When she returned to the front room, the cat was sat in her husband's old chair again, warming by the fire. She smiled at the scene, reminded of her own Arthur who would snooze away on long afternoons in that spot. She set the saucer on the floor and after a while the cat jumped down to have a taste, before returning to the chair and its comfort. Closing its eyes in a slumbering fashion.

Mrs. Macready then went about her usual morning routine. She ate some breakfast herself, she got changed and went into the back garden to get some more logs of the fire. She pottered about her house and watered the plants that needed a drink, then she began to bake a tea-loaf that she would munch on in the afternoon with her tea and read her magazine.

And the cat remained in the chair.

Of course, the weather didn't help matters. The wind continued to howl, and the rain poured all day. Only once did the cat come to investigate what she was up to. Sniffing about the kitchen when the cake was in the oven. She fed it a few bits of chicken from the fridge, and it returned to the chair again where it resided all day.

"Humph, you *are* a lazy one aren't you!" she said to the cat, coming in to stoke the fire and remove the empty saucer of milk. "Not much of a companion really, are you?" she added. The cat stared at her, then began to lick its paws absently.

"You'll eat me out of house and home before long with all this milk and chicken," she said, going back to the fridge to top up the little saucer once more for the cat.

Soon the afternoon faded, and evening fell away too, and it was time to go to bed. The storm still raged outside, one of the trees across the way in the horse field fell over she noticed, while the others were pummeled by the wind and the rain. She decided to let the cat stay inside overnight. Wherever it had come from, to return now would be too cruel to be sent back out into the tempest.

She patted the cat's head as it remained in the chair it had clung to all day and she sifted the dying embers in the fire with the poker before saying goodnight and going upstairs to bed.

— — —

She woke the next day to find the cat at the bottom of her own bed, curled up asleep. She could hear it purring away in a deep slumber and she was very quiet making her way to the bathroom. The storm had blown itself out, and a stillness surrounded her little cottage once more. She went downstairs to get a glass of water as her throat was itchy and dry.

Coming to the bottom of the stairs she noticed a small bit of fluff on the floor. A little white cloud on the vast black slate sea. She picked it up and inspected it, she then noticed another bit by the door that led into the living room. Following the cloud breadcrumbs, she entered the room and was confronted by a definition for chaos. The cushions had been clawed at, their contents spilling out in a final bow of defeat, then spread around the room in a scattered frenzy. There were claw marks up the chair the cat had sat on all day, and cat poo by the fire. She could smell the feces, cooked slightly as the fireplace had spread its dying warmth throughout the night over the tiles that surrounded it.

'Right,' she thought and marched up to her bedroom to confront the beast.

She found that cat had nestled itself into her bed now, leaving the end of the bed to now lie within the covers. It had curled itself up against the duvet and was purring away again as if in some wonderful dream.

"Come on you. Out now." Mrs. Macready said entering the room and spotting where the cat had moved to. She waggled the duvet to wake it up and clapped her hands to surprise it. The cat slowly opened its eyes and yawned, unimpressed by the loud creature making a fuss and waving its hands.

She dove into the covers and picked the cat up, marching it out of the bedroom and down the stairs.

"The rain has stopped, and you've out-stayed your welcome. So now out!" she said, fumbling with the front door with the cat in hand. She eventually got the latch open and plonked the cat outside on her welcome mat. It sat there and turned its head, first to the garden which hung with a wetness from all the rain, then back at Mrs. Macready, as if silently saying 'You don't expect me to go out *there*, do you?'

"Now don't give me that look. You've ruined my front room, and it's time you were off. So, go on, get going," she said, nudging the cat with her foot.

The cat remained.

She sighed and threw her hands in the air.

"Suit yourself," she said to the cat and hurried inside herself, mindful the cat did not dart its way in as she closed the door again.

Some time passed, and she checked outside again: the cat was still there on her mat. He hadn't moved. She went about her usual activities, checking sporadically if the feline had shifted. "Stubborn!" she said, peering out of the front window. She let it sit there all day, not encouraging it or bringing it any treats.

She went to bed that night with the cat still sitting on her porch.

It was around two in the morning when she heard the noise. The meowing and clawing was almost deafening. It came from the back of the house and she sat up in her bed with a start. She looked at her clock and was shaken with a memory of her husband Arthur coming home drunk in the early morning, waking her and the neighbors.

She flew out of bed and down to the backdoor. She grabbed her broom which she kept propped against her cupboard and opened the door. The cat had been scratching at the wood, claw marks could be seen where it had frantically tried to get inside.

"That's enough now!" she said to the cat, as it tried to come inside but was blocked by her agile broom technique. "Now, away with you," she said, nudging the cat with her broom. The cat failed to be moved. It lay down and looked up at her in an imploring fashion.

Mrs. Macready was struck suddenly by the sadness in the cat's eyes. She sighed to herself and closed the door, going across to the fridge and retrieving the milk bottle out and the little saucer yet again. She opened the door once more and put the saucer down by the cat.

"Now, have some of this and be off. They'll be no more, so don't think I'm being weak in this regard." She poured the milk out generously into the saucer where it sploshed over the sides; the cat licked at the drops that had spilled out onto the ground. Just as she had sorted her husband out in his own drunken states, getting him water and putting him to bed, she did the same with the cat; propping one of the ruined cushions by the little log shed she had by her back door. It was dry here, and she had set a boundary of not having the cat in the house. She patted it once again on the head and closed the door.

The meowing and scratching had ceased, and Mrs. Macready went back to bed, happy in the knowledge she had done a nice thing.

ESCALATE

She had a bird-spotting book which she kept on the little shelf near the toaster in the kitchen. It was an old frail thing, falling apart; much like herself, she thought as she would thumb through it, eager to find out what kind of bird she had just witnessed swooping into her garden to peck at the coconut shells she had hanging from the trees. She would often grab the book in a hurry, not trusting her memory to get the correct plumage color or size of the bird that had graced her garden with its presence. She liked spotting her feathered little friends and looked forward to the winter months when she would be able to spot the robins more; their bright red breast like a crushed berry against the frosted ground.

It was a sparrow, and a young one; she could tell that right away. The poor little fledging had been snuffed of its life before it had time to soar in the skies.

The bird lay on the bristled doormat by her backdoor. The cat sat nearby, proud of its handiwork and perhaps expectant of some grand reward. The small lifeless creature had some ruffled feathers around its neck, and some blood had already dried on its body. Little red spots indicated the puncture wounds from the cat's spear-like teeth. It happened suddenly, her eyes filled with tears as she bent down and picked up the dead bird. She lifted it carefully in her hands and made her way out into the garden. She did not look at the cat or acknowledge it was there. Inside she was caught between anger and sorrow, the wave of sadness washing her insides while the cliffs of anger loomed.

She picked up a small trowel she had in one of her garden buckets that she kept near the greenhouse and ventured off down the path to find a quiet spot under the weeping willow tree that cascaded along the ridge of her garden boundary.

She dug a little hole and placed the bird down inside, snapping off a bit of the tree that hung silently above her. She put this over the bird and began to pull the soil over the little grave, patting it down once she was done. She knew it was the cycle of nature and that these things happened, but she was still very upset that this had happened in her little space. Her little slice of Eden now had a serpent to contend with. There was something she had sensed in the cat that made her believe that it did it to spite her. Something in the eyes. Her husband would often have done little things around the house that he knew wound her up. He seemed to take a certain satisfaction to her annoyance at times, and she sensed that also in the cat. Silly really, she thought. She didn't have notions of reincarnation or any of that nonsense, but the cat somehow reminded her of Arthur; both the good and the bad.

The cat, grown curious by the activity by the tree, had joined her, and brushed up against her leg before prancing over to the freshly disturbed soil. It sniffed and pawed at the freshly dug earth, seemingly eager to get at the bird once more as a final insult. Disturbing its resting place.

Swiftly, with her own cat-like reflexes, Mrs. Macready swung her leg back and threw it forward with all her might; grinding her teeth together as her foot made contact with the cat and sent it flying halfway across the garden.

"You nasty little brute!" she yelled as the cat screeched over the grass, landing naturally on its feet some distance away. She then bent down and picked up some stones, lobbing them in the cat's direction.

"Get out of here, out! You stay out of my garden now, you vicious little bastard," she called, throwing the stones and sending the cat racing from her garden and over the small fence into the fields beyond. She returned to the little grave and placed a bigger stone over the soil, wedging it down into the dark ground. She straightened up and headed back towards the house muttering to herself, wiping away tiny tears.

"That little shit. I can take a lot, but that's too far. Arthur incarnate he is, I remember he would bring birds back also and he would get a right walloping too." She turned on the spot and called to where she had seen the cat race away, "And let that be a warning to you!" she said, shaking her finger in the air.

She made her way back up the little path towards her door, completely forgetting the reason she had come outside in the first place. Once back inside, she popped the kettle on and made herself a strong coffee, adding in a nip of whisky 'to keep the cold out'.

FAREWELL

She heard it now, a clattering in the garden. She knew it was the cat; she had seen it about an hour ago as she'd passed the window and looked out into the front garden. It had been on the wall, walking towards the house. She had been keeping an eye out for the postman and had spotted the ginger creature bopping along the wall.

The noise came again, like large metal trays were tumbling onto the ground. It was those old trays she used for her plant pots, the ones she had picked up at the local jumble to use for her gardening. 'He must be by the small shed' she thought. She tried to ignore it all, but the noises were coming with frequency. She made her way to the kitchen and put on the wellingtons that she kept by the back door. It had rained again that morning and she knew the ground would be muddy and wet.

She opened the back door and went to step outside but noticed something again on her mat. He heart sank like a weighted stone. She was lost for words, even the anger took its time to bubble up inside her. There on her mat lay three small ducklings, their little yellow and brown feathers fluffed in the trauma of their encounter with the cat. Their heads all slumped to the same side as their lives had cruelly been ended. The cat which was now in her little shed causing no end of noise and commotion.

Mrs. Macready stepped over the dead little birds and stormed towards the shed. The cat had snuck in through a small hole on the side. It was an old wooden shed with a huge glass skylight. Her husband had built it years ago with the idea of using it as a greenhouse, before buying a proper one to replace it, which stood itself further off down the garden. She kept a lot of junk in the shed, and most of it was stacked precariously on top of itself. The noises she heard were the sounds of things tumbling onto the floor.

She slid the latch open and pulled the door forth. There was a flash of ginger and the cat darted behind the old lawnmower. She could smell the mix of old potting soil and cat piss and noticed a puddle by the spades and rakes where the cat had gone.

"Come out you little bugger, enough is enough now!" she yelled into the shed. She began to paw at the items inside, not caring for those things that came toppling her way. She heaved boxes and old plant pots to the side in a frantic state to get to the cat. She saw it dart again and again away from her, almost teasingly. She heard it whine and whimper as it sped around the shed, sending more and more items her way. A basket which she kept on one of the top shelves was dislodged by the cat as it moved past it and came crashing down onto her head. The basket itself was not heavy, but inside she had stored trowels and gardening tools, one of which flung itself up out of the confines of the basket and grazed her forehead causing her to bleed. She stepped back suddenly, caught by the little item and surprised momentarily.

As she stood back, the cat made its move.

Quick as a flash, the cat sprang out of the dark recess it had been hiding. Its claws bared and teeth sharp, it launched itself onto her face, scratching and tearing at her skin. It hissed and slashed at her as she tried to prize it off her. She did not cry or scream out in alarm. It had not been the first time she had been attacked or surprised by some danger. She had grown resourceful and strong over the years living with Arthur, taking those fights as a silent victim and burying the resentment down deep.

She punched the cat in the side, her knuckles penetrating deep into the fur where she could feel its ribs. The cat, caught off guard, fell from her face and onto the floor; landing on its back in a daze.

It was here when she was swift.

She stepped on its paw heavily, trapping it under her boot and reached for the spade which had remained, despite the commotion, propped up against the side. Without any hesitation she lifted it quickly into the air and brought it down with a heavy force onto of the cat's head with hard thunk as the metal hit the bone. Years of resentment, pain and guilt lifted and struck the spade time and again onto the cat until much of it was squashed into the floor of the shed.

— — —

A light drizzle was coating her hands now as she heaved the last bit of soil across and patted it down. The little grave for the cat was way down at the bottom of the garden, hidden away under the shadows of a douglas fir tree.

"I'm sorry it came to this my little friend, but you had it coming after all your antics," she said. Her knees dug deep into the ground and she could feel the water on her legs as she knelt on the wet grass.

"There's only so much I can take, and you pushed things too far," she said again to the silence. She reached across and picked a small stone up, placing it down over the little grave as a marker. She rose then and reached up to the tree, snapping off two bits of the branch with nice leafy ends. She bent down and placed one of them into the ground where the cat had been buried, like a little bunch of flowers. She stepped across to where a much larger stone rested also under the tree and placed the other little branch into the ground and then stood back.

"Still, you two weren't all bad," she said, before turning and making her way back towards her little cottage, heading inside to wash her hands and make a warm cup of tea.

THE TRUTH LIES IN DARKNESS

by Bobby Blade

Tommy watched them playing outside his bedroom window that morning. He observed how they huddled together, excitement and adrenaline running through them. Plastic soldiers dressed in camouflage and equipped with tactical gear, dug down in their makeshift muddy trenches, overlooking the patchy, sun-baked grass, for any enemies lurking beyond. Each one had his miniature rifle; some propped in position, ready to fire. Others slung across their backs. Tommy heard the 'booms' and 'bangs' from the imaginary rounds being shot off, all imaginatively mouthed by the group of children.

One of those boys, Curtis Higgins, looked up at Tommy, who jumped out of sight, attempting to go unnoticed. He did not succeed. When he worked up the nerve to look down again, Curtis stood with a derisive smile, flipping him the bird. He receded back inside, shutting the blinds.

Nice going, twinkle-toes, he told himself, making his way to the bed. He sat on the edge of the mattress, reflecting. He hated Curtis Higgins. Ever since he moved into the neighborhood, he'd always found a way to crawl under his skin.

Him and all his magnificent toys.

Tommy didn't have such luxuries. In fact, he didn't possess much of anything. All he had was Roxy, his lullaby-singing bear. Tattered, its brown polyester fur, worn and faded. Red overalls, with a large musical note on the bib, once lit up and played a soothing tune when pressed. Tommy would never get to hear one, he had acquired it in poor condition, broken of its internal voice box.

It made no difference, he loved it just the same.

It wasn't gifted to him, nor did he wake up to it, covered in green and gold wrapping paper, waiting for him under the Christmas tree. Their very first encounter came two months earlier, on a hot sunny day.

— — —

"Tommy!" Calvin cried. "That waste-heap isn't going to toss itself out. Get your butt out here, now!"

The bedroom door swung open. Tommy rushed out, hopping on one leg, slipping on his sneaker. He reached the living room where his father sat on a lazy-boy, feet propped-up on the coffee table, a chilled Budweiser in his hand. The baseball game was on, Baltimore led 3-0 in the bottom of the 4th inning.

"You called?" he said, panting.

"Yes, I did! Did you forget that we have chores in this house? The trashcan is overflowing like a goddamn volcano in the kitchen! Throw it out and change the bag."

Immediately, Tommy dashed into the kitchen. "Sorry Dad, I must have forgotten."

"Forgotten? You aren't going to forget this knuckle sandwich I'm about to give you, if you don't get moving!" Tommy pulled and zipped the garbage bag tight, thrusting it over his back, starting for the front door.

"...and hurry it up!" he continued. "I need you to bring me another Bud from the fridge when you're done!"

Tommy carted the trash up the sloped path where the wastebins were located. He grimaced against the sun beaming down into his eyes, setting the bag at the base of the metal containers. The large plastic hood exploded with buzzing flies when Tommy lifted it. Recoiling at the stench, and at the buzzards pecking his ears, he threw the lid up as hard as he could, where it balanced momentarily, before slamming back against the steel. The garbage went into the container, releasing a foul odor, Tommy covered his mouth and nose, gagging at the smell making its way down his nostrils.

And that's when he first saw him.

Half-buried between browning vegetation and a greasy Domino's Pizza box; Roxy's feet poked out among the rubbish. Tommy's eyes widened. Leaping halfway inside, balancing at waist level, he stretched out his hand, reaching for one foot. Planting his two feet back on solid ground, he pulled out his future best friend, filthy and pungent. He shook off the remnants of decaying salad and smiled ecstatically.

Aside from its age, it was all there; arms, legs, eyes and clothing. He had a large tear down the side of its body, which he assumed, was the reason for it being discarded. Clumps of cotton protruded out, he quickly jabbed it back in with two fingers.

"Tommy!" His father called out from a distance.

At once, Tommy gave him another shake, before stuffing it under his shirt and sprinting home.

"Where the hell have you been?" Calvin said, an unlit cigarette between his lips. He smacked Tommy in the back of the head as he ran past him and into the house. "I've been calling you for some time, do you have problems with your hearing too?"

Tommy stood with his back to him, trying to hide his excitement, arms down in front of him. "No sir," he said. "The bag tore, and everything spilled out onto the concrete. I had to scoop it into the dumpster by hand."

Nice one, he thought, impressed by his own quick thinking.

Lighting the Marlboro and drawing in the toxins, Calvin exhaled the plume of smoke, after a much-needed dose of nicotine. "Not only deaf, but clumsy?" A series of hard phlegm coughs followed. "You sure take after your mother, I guess stupid IS contagious." He chuckled, starting for the recliner.

"Sorry Dad," he said, defeated. "I'll get that beer for you now."

"Ah, shit, I already got it! Did you think I was going to sit around, waiting for your lazy ass to fetch it whenever you saw fit?"

"No sir," Tommy said, instinctively.

"Now, replace that bag, and scram to do whatever it is you do."

"Yes sir!" He waddled suspiciously into the kitchen.

"Wait a minute! Come here. What do you have under there?"

Tommy paused and swallowed. "What?"

"I said, what are you hiding? Don't act dumb with me. Out with it!"

Reluctantly, he raised his shirt, exposing a furry ball sticking out from under it. He held it out in his hands, head down, and eyes towards the floor.

"What the hell is that? Is that what I think it is?" He snatched it away from his grasp and inspected it. "Just what were you planning to do with this?"

"It was in the dumpster. I didn't steal it, honest! I was going to clean it, and..."

"And what? Keep it?" He straightened in his chair. "Behind my back?" Tommy diverted his eyes away from him and down the hallway.

"Don't look for your mother," he scolded him. "She isn't here! Now, tell me!"

Tommy teared up, not knowing what to do or say. Calvin reached over, grabbing him around the arm, pulling him close.

"What did I say about crying like a little sissy? Wipe them tears off before I slap them off!" Tommy quickly ran his sleeve across both eyes.

"Now, answer my godda-" The door opened.

Jenny walked in, groceries weighing heavily on her fingers. Calvin let go of him, nudging him back a step.

"Don't you ever come into this house with something you don't deserve, you hear me, you little shit?" He snickered at him. "Now, get the hell out of my sight!" He flung Roxy across the room to the couch on the other end. Tommy broke into a sob, ran down the hall, bumped into his mother, and disappeared into his room.

"What's going on?" Jenny said, concerned. "What's wrong with Tommy?"

"Nothing," he said, reclining back. "Lying like always, trying to sneak that filthy plush into his room." She looked at Roxy laying on the cushion, then back at him.

"It's just a teddy-bear. And he's just a little boy."

"You know what Jen? That's why he acts the way he does, all faggy and sissified! If you keep shielding him from becoming a man, how the hell is he going to get through this life, cowering behind a woman's skirt?"

"Because he is my son," she exclaimed. "And he's only ten years old! Kids cry when their feelings get hurt, Calvin. They desire to play with teddy bears! What is wrong with you?" She released the bags, sending them crashing. She turned furiously and walked away. He watched her leave, dismissed her, and knocked back another drink.

Later that evening, Jenny entered Tommy's room. He laid on his side, sniffling. She sat next to him, placing her hand lovingly on his shoulder. "Baby boy? Are you okay?"

"No," he said, softly. He wrapped the pillow over his face.

"I have something for you," she whispered. "Turn around and have a peek."

Rolling over, sluggishly, he noticed Roxy in her mother's hands. He had been scrubbed clean; his torn side sewn shut. He glanced at his mother.

"Here." She said, handing it to him. "Take him."

He looked down at him, feeling his damp fur. "I... I can keep him?"

"You can keep him," she assured him. Holding him in his arms, still not convinced, he gave him a hard squeeze, which soon erased all doubts. Then he dove into his mother's arms, embracing her.

133

"Thank you, mama. Thank you!"

She drew him closer. "You're welcome, baby boy, I love you."

Tommy sat on the edge of the bed, reminiscing, with a wide smile on his face.

That afternoon, Curtis Higgins eleventh birthday celebration was well underway. Blue and red streamers spread out like spider webs throughout the back patio. Helium-filled balloons swayed in the summer breeze. Children gathered around Curtis, as he removed a large red bow from his brand-new bicycle. Tommy heard the 'ooohs' and 'aaaahs' from the energized boys and girls, as he ripped open one present after another. He sat perched atop a masonry wall in the distance, Roxy sitting by his side. He had not been asked to attend, and though he did not care to join in on the festivities of someone he loathed, he could not push away the strong sting of rejection.

Leaping off the edge, the impact of his soles touching the grade, creating small dust-clouds. Dusting himself off, he started for home. Midway, he heard spinning spokes and metal chains approaching. Distant panting and laughter accompanied treads skidding against concrete. A shiny aluminum frame, black with gold accents, slammed on its footbrakes; the smell of new rubber drifted into the air. It was Curtis Higgins and his band of goons.

"Hey, Tommy?" He said, catching his breath. "I bet my bike can out-race your bike on any given day!" He waited for his words to marinate. "Oh, that's right, you don't have one!" He ridiculed him. The rest of the group instantly joining in.

Curtis observed Roxy, dangling from Tommy's hand. "Aren't you a little too old to play with dolls?" He examined him further. "...and an ugly one at that!" They teased him some more.

Tommy ground his teeth.

"See you later, twerp!" Pedaling and gaining momentum, Curtis started downhill. His trained seals trailed after him. Tommy watched them disappear around the corner, regretting not defending himself.

"Don't listen to him," a familiar voice said. "He does that to everyone. Besides, you can borrow my bike anytime you want. I don't mind."

"Thanks Carlos," Tommy said.

Carlos Vega was Tommy's only friend on Bradbury Street, up until he moved three blocks away, two years before. He stopped by, occasionally, for a friendly game of hide-and-seek, or to attend a special occasion, like he had that day. His friendship with Curtis was a decent one. But after a while, his self-indulgence, got to be too much. Opting-out from the ride-a-long, he decided to head home early for supper.

"Nice! Does it talk?"

"Nah, not anymore. His voice box is all busted-up. But he's still kind of cool to have around." Carlos passed Roxy an indifferent gaze.

"Yeah, I guess. Anyway, here, I swiped you a goodie-bag from Curtis's house. He won't miss it. They have buckets of them." He placed it in Tommy's hand.

"Thanks. But...I can't. I'm not allowed to have any sweets at my house. My father will have a fit!" Peering inside the bag, he scooped out some sour patch kids, before handing it back.

"I'll just manage with these for now." Popping them into his mouth, he smiled at him, mischievously. They giggled in unison and said their farewells.

"Roxy, let's go find something to do in our room." He chewed quickly, swallowed, picked and licked his teeth, getting rid of any visible evidence, before they reached the front door.

Back in his room, Roxy sat on the bed, propped up by two pillows. Tommy scanned the closet for something they could pass the time with. On the floor, tucked deep in a corner, a blue shoe-box grabbed his attention. Pushing off a stack of old comics that weighed down the lid, he took it up on his lap. Inside, the box revealed mostly school supplies. Among the pencils, rulers and erasers, Tommy spotted a clear zip-lock bag, with about half a dozen hot wheels piled together.

"Bingo!" he exclaimed. "Roxy, check this out! I forgot all about the-"

Turning, the zip-lock bag slipped from his grasp. The sound of steel and plastic bouncing off the hardwood flooring, echoed through the small room. The goodie-bag rested on the comforter, half-spilled, beside Roxy. It was the same one Carlos had given to him.

"How did that get there?" He raced over to it, picking it up and quickly began cramming everything back inside. He had to put it out of sight before his fa-

The door opened. Calvin stumbled in, balancing himself against the door casing. A six-pack of Budweisers swirling in his gut, a newly opened one cupped in his hand.

"What have I told you about leaving your sneakers lying around?"

Tommy stood in the center of the room, holding the stuffed goodie-bag. Calvin's demeanor altered, his intoxication, stirring within. Fumbling to him, he ripped the bag away.

"What the hell is this?"

Immobilized, Tommy was overcome with fear.

"I... I don't know," he said, petrified. "I haven't the slightest idea. I didn't bring it in, honest I didn't!"

Calvin took him by the arm and shook him. "Don't lie to me! Do you really think I'm dumb enough to believe that shit? What have I told you about sneaking this crap into the house?"

Tommy's eyes flooded, breaking into a tremor. He tried responding to his father, but the words did not find their way out. His pant leg began to spot, as a steady flow of urine trickled down and puddled by his foot.

"Answer me when I talk to you, you little brat!" He threw him backwards on the bed. Roxy bounced a few times, falling over the side. The goodie-bag exploded against the wall, sending its contents sprawling to the floor. He placed the Budweiser on the dresser and began undoing his belt.

"You must be craving a whipping! Alright, then. I'll give you a whipping. One you won't soon forget!" With a final jerk, the leather strap came loose. Wrapping one end in a fist, smacking the other, hard against the mattress. At the impact, Tommy scurried to the other end of the bed.

He began to cry.

Raising his hand high, the thick hide came down on the boy's side. His screams boomed throughout the house, reaching Jenny, who was in the kitchen preoccupied over dinner. At his cries, she sprinted to his bedroom. Upon entering, she found Tommy curled up in a fetal-position, his arms welted and red from blocking the blows. Repeatedly, Calvin struck him, landing the whip wherever it pleased. Jenny placed herself between the two, taking hold of his arm, halting him.

"Stop!" She cried. "You're hurting him!" She wrestled to secure the leather belt, but Cal was too blind with anger to give it up.

"Get the hell out of my way, you stupid cunt!" A backhand landed across her jaw, sending her flying back against the dresser. The Budweiser tipped over and rolled off the edge.

He stopped at the sight of her body rebounding off the dresser's exterior. Taking deep breaths, he towered over both, crying in pain. Jenny supported her jaw, a stream of blood flowing from her nose. The Budweiser gushed out onto the wood slats, bleeding into the crevices. Tommy's screams, now reduced to painful whimpers and sporadic sighs, muffled deep into his pillow. All he kept telling himself was *drift away, please drift away, anywhere - but here!*

Calvin had taken his temper to a new level. The scenario had crossed his mind, during countless, heated rants, but he'd always managed to control himself from such acts. Now, those very acts, had come and gone. Nothing he did could reverse them. His instincts told him to go to her, hold her and apologize. He could feel the immense guilt washing over him. But his ego would not let him, it would not drift to its currents.

"Look at what you've made me do!" He said, disguising the sudden onslaught of remorse. Stepping over her, he picked up the empty can. "You made me drop my beer." He went silent, exiting the room without saying another word. Jenny rose and closed the door, securing the locking mechanism on the knob. She wrapped her arms around her son, carefully, tending to his wounds.

They wept for a long time.

— — —

That night, all was silent throughout the house. Jenny sat in the bedroom, looking out of the window to an empty street. Eyeliner streaked down to her jawline as a testament of her abuse. Her stare was dead. Sharp pains pounded her temples, her nose crusted with rings of dried blood. The door opened, Calvin entered, cautiously.

"Jen?" he said, apologetically. "Can I talk to you?" There was no reply. "Please, I know you're sore at me, but I need to say something."

After no reply, he said, "Well, I'm going to say it anyway, and I need you to listen." He took a seat opposite to her. "I'm sorry. Believe me, I don't know what came over me! I mean, I do know. My drinking, it's a problem." He waited for a reaction but got none. "My temper," he continued. "It gets out of hand here and there."

She gave him a nasty look but did not say a word.

"But I would never hurt you. Not like that."

She listened to the man that spoke but did not grasp the words being spoken. He experienced a guilt-trip for belting her and sending her airborne across the room. He did not grow a conscience, suddenly, and discover the many errors of his ways. He knew she would not tolerate this degree of abuse from him. She had enough; the name-calling, the raging fits and strict rules. But for all the yelling and punching holes in the walls, he'd never laid a hand on her. She blamed herself in part. She met him that way. Embittered and angry from his own upbringing, she decided to love him, regardless of his innumerable tantrums and broken knick-knacks he was accustomed to throwing. For each one, she'd always tell herself that he would change.

But not when it came to Tommy. Not her baby boy. What made it worse, Tommy's name never came out in the entirety of his nonsensical babbling. It sickened her.

"Have you forgotten Tommy?" she said. "The damage you've done to your son?" He looked away, abashed. He had not entered his mind.

"I... I mean, I give him a scolding occasionally," he said. "We must teach him a lesson. He can't run around breaking all the rules!" He drew closer. "I do it for his own good. Believe me, Jenny, I do!"

Calmly, she said, "I've put up with your temper and abuse for a long time, Calvin. Not for the *stupid cunt* you see me as, but for the love I have for you. I've swallowed your lies, obeyed your rules and allowed you to disparage Tommy, for the sake of your so-called disciplinary measures. In your delusional mind, he's not worthy of a simple teddy bear. God forbid he brings candy into this house, for fear of getting slashed like some damn animal!"

His eyes went downcast.

"I heard you," she went on. "Now, listen to me: if you ever lay your hands on us again, I promise you, you'll regret it!"

Sensing possible reconciliation, he knelt beside her, taking her hand.

"I swear, Jen, I promise you, it will never ha-"

She jerked her hand away. "You said everything you came to say. You heard all I am going to say. Now, it's time for you to leave." Her words dug deep into him. She closed herself off completely. He would not get another word off. He got to his feet and took his leave.

Tommy heard every word his mother said to his father. A tear escaped as he smiled to himself in his moon-lit room. He hugged Roxy, wiping his wet cheek on his fur. His love for his mother multiplied at that moment. But he did not believe his father meant what he said to her. He'd heard it all before.

And that scared him greatly.

— — —

Calvin opened his eyes. They grew wide in the darkness of night.

His heart rate elevated, his breathing became erratic. He strained his muscles, struggling to move. He was paralyzed - both in fear and body. He had passed out on the lazy-boy, shortly after his conversation with Jenny. After that night, he assumed he'd sleep on it for some time. He accepted that. Wasting no time, he drooped down into it, sulking, unable to forget Jenny's words. He drank the last of his beer, staring at the family portrait above the mantelpiece. It depicted happier times, long smiles captured for all time, but felt foreign and odd. He spent hours trying to pinpoint where things went wrong. The last thing that ran through his mind before drifting off into unconsciousness, was how bad he needed another beer.

He had lucked out in that department.

The moonlight cast its light through the half-opened blinds. The grandfather clock resonated, playing its famous rendition of 'tick-tock', while outside, the neighbor's cat meowed and wailed on top of the wooden fence that ran along the front lawn.

Then, he heard the footsteps.

Rolling his eyes into his head, attempting to see who paced behind, all he could make out was black. He shouted, calling out to Jenny, who slept in their bed, bruised and desolate. But no one heard him. No audible sound escaped. All his screams took place inside his head.

"Hello, Cal," a voice hissed. The tone was low and menacing, sending a dreadful chill down his unmoving bones. It laughed, amused, sensing his distress.

"What's the matter? The *stupid cunt* can't hear you anymore?" It laughed again, gingerly stroking his forehead. Although he could not move, there was no denying the scorching finger tracing across his perspiring brow. It burned and sizzled against the sweat. A figure emerged, tall and cloaked in black. It slithered effortlessly through the room, ghostlike. It had no distinguishable features, just an abyss of darkness with no end. It descended, taking a seat on the coffee table in front of him. Cal stared directly at it, gazing deep into its desolation. The figure stared back, deep into his fear and trepidation.

Who are you? Calvin thought. *What do you want?*

The figure smiled, revealing sharp, rotting fangs. Hundreds of them! They were stacked on top of one another, ready to strike. Beyond them, in the void, a long tongue that smoldered like lava, rattled with evil intent. Two fiery eyes materialized out of nothing and burned bright.

"Who am I?" The figure said, reading his thoughts. "I'm your worst nightmare!" A blazing hand reached across and seized Calvin around the neck. His flesh began to cook against the grills of its fingers. The smell of burning flesh rose, tantalizing the figures appetite. Calvin's body remained immobilized, but his agonizing screams reverberated within him. He thrashed in silent convulsions. The hand retracted, leaving behind charred markings on his neck's surface.

Please. Somebody help me! Jenny? Tommy?

"Jenny? Tommy?" he said, taunting. "*Now* you cry out to those you've hurt for so long. And now, you find yourself the victim." It leaned forward, placing a hand on top of his lap. Another searing pain shot through him.

"Now you will feel pain. You will feel sorrow, and torture will rule over you for eternities to come!"

Please stop! For the love of god, STOP!

"Isn't that what Jenny asked of you? When you beat your son mercilessly and without remorse?"

I'm sorry. I'm sorry, but please, stop burning me! The pain is too great!

"Exactly like the pain she felt when you disfigured her nose?" It lunged forward and clamped down on his nose with its sharp teeth, tearing it off completely. His screams were terrified, blood spewed out, ran down, seeping back into his mouth. The figure chewed on his flesh with great hunger, watching him squirm and on the edge of fainting. Calvin was re-awakened with a hot, probing finger to the side of his ribs.

"Did you enjoy the lashes you rained down on your son? That's how your father used to beat you, isn't it? Remember the night he came home drunk as a skunk? You were what, ten, eleven years old? Right around Tommy's age. You were on the floor, playing with your soldier men. He walked through the front door, stumbling over himself. Your mother, sustained him, guiding him to his seat, keeping him from falling over. He stepped on a pile of your little green men. Do you remember what he said to you?"

'God-dammit, Calvin, what have I told you about leaving your shit lying around the house!'

"Remember how he kicked them from your little hands? Your mother, bless her heart, tried to avoid another one of his intoxicated meltdowns, ushering him past you, enticing him with another drink. But you just had to start weeping, didn't you? Who could blame you? All you cared about was playing with soldier men, having sweet treats and riding your bicycle with the neighborhood kids. Remember how he ridiculed you as you wept?"

'Stop your crying, you little shit! Did I have a son, or some fagotty-sissy-girl?'

"He lifted you up by the arm and shook you, violently, so that you pissed all over yourself. Your mother tried to pry him off you, but she only caught the other end of his wrath."

"Stop!" Calvin cried. "No more, please, STOP IT! I don't want to hear anymore!"

"I'm afraid you must hear what I have to say. And you will listen! Where was I? Ah, yes, the beatings. The beating he gave your mother that night. He tossed her across the living room, sending her against the bookcase. He kicked her in her stomach, repeatedly, snapping her ribcage."

Cal's eyes welled up.

"Then, he turned his rage on you. Oh, how you screamed, those terrible sounds! You ran from him, as he chased you into the bedroom. You tried shutting the door, only to have it cave in from a heavy boot. You dragged yourself across the floor to the other end, crying for your mother, who never came. Pinning you down with his knees, his heavy hands wailed down across your face, not stopping until you passed out from the pain. Remember?"

Enough! Yes, Yes, I remember it all too well. I'm so sorry.

He wept without ceasing.

"You'll be sorry, alright! And you'll hurt much more where you're going, buddy boy! You'll never see Jenny or Tommy again. You'll never hurt them with your spiteful words!"

Who...what are you?

The faceless figure hovered over him.

"You can call me..."

His mouth expanded; sharp teeth came down, feasting on every part of him. The chair shook violently, his body thrashed back and forth like a rag doll. It went on like that for a long time. All in the darkness of night.

— — —

In the morning, Jenny walked out of the room, wrapped in her robe. There was something wrong in the air. She couldn't place her finger on it. But she knew something wasn't right. On the dining room floor, glass lay broken and scattered. Wooden picture frames lay twisted and disfigured, attached only by the staples that held it together. She wondered how she slept through another one of Calvin's destructions. Chairs were overturned, every drawer was pulled opened. Broken plates and utensils littered the floor.

Jenny stood over one photograph; a family picture of them taken three Christmases ago, in front of her sister's house. The image was torn, half of it turned over, exposing the watermarks from the film developer. The other, showed Jenny smiling, her arm around a younger Tommy, who looked off to the side. Calvin was on the other half of the image, torn from view. After a moment, she stepped over it, and started towards the living room.

The recliner faced away from her; she could see the top of his head over the headrest. His right arm hung down; his grip twisted in place. She approached him, carefully. When she reached the lazy-boy, Calvin lay in his chair, his left arm on his lap. His blue mechanics uniform was drenched in sweat, his eyes wide open, fixed towards the ceiling. His mouth stretched open, as if trying to speak; purple lips contrasting against his pale skin. His chest no longer rose or fell.

He was dead.

He had been for some time. A heart attack, she thought. Too much alcohol finally did him in. She had always pushed away the thoughts of such scenarios, cringing at how she would feel, act or respond to such a reality. But there she stood, calm and void of any emotion. It was nowhere near the way she imagined it.

She watched him for a long time.

Then, her eyes shifted, examining the devastation around the room. On the couch, resting on his side, *Roxy stared up at her.*

GRIMM

by M. Ennenbach

"It does not matter in the slightest what a review says about your place, Ms. Levine. If you cannot pay the rent on the store we will have to see that a tenant who can, takes it."

Dana stared at the phone in her hand. She wanted to reach through and strangle the bastard on the other end. She knew he was just doing his job. It wasn't his fault she was two months behind on the rent. She'd overstretched her resources. Believed her friends that raved about her cupcakes. Let them convince her that she had what it takes to thrive in an industry that had long passed its boom. She found the perfect location not far from the train station. Sure, it was pricey. Too pricey. But the morning commuters and word of mouth would spread, and she'd be back in the black before long.

"I understand. I just need this review to be published. Once people read it they will flock in. I know it."

"Be that as it may, you are hereby on notice. A third month in arrears and your lease agreement in terminated. You need to stay ahead of this or by this time next month, your store will be closed."

"I understand. Thank you. I'll send a payment as soon as possible."

"I hope you do. Good day, Ms. Levine."

"Same to you sir." She looked at the phone. Saw the call end. "FUCK!"

She was in trouble. Deep. She knew it too. She didn't need off-hand threats.

"If you don't pay me, I'll come down there and repossess your smug fucking smile. You won't like that much, will you? Probably drive a nice sports car. Slash your fucking tires…"

The bell to the front door chimed and she cut herself off mid-rant. She brushed her apron smooth and plastered a smile on to her face and stepped into the front of the shop. "Welcome to Dana Cakes! What can I get you today? The German chocolate are oven fresh!"

She frowned. There was no one there. She looked all around the small entrance and didn't see a single person. "I must be hearing things. I swore that was the front door."

She looked at her phone and saw it was eight fifteen. The big rush was occurring right outside the door. People walked with a purpose down the crowded sidewalk. All heading to the train station. Yet, not a single one entered the shop. One well dressed man stopped and stared into the window. She put on her best grin. Then watched in horror as he picked his nose, examined it, then smeared it onto the brick next to the plate glass. He noticed her and the look of disgust on her face before smiling and continuing on down the street.

"What the fuck?"

"Ahem."

She nearly jumped out of her skin in fright. Someone *had* entered the shop. And was standing at the counter. No. Beneath. She got on her tip toes and looked down at him. He was a dwarf, maybe three and a half feet tall. She flushed scarlet.

"I am so sorry. I didn't see you…"

"It's quite alright, madam."

"What can I get for you, sir? Pick any cupcake and I'll give you one on the house. The lemon is my bestseller. The chocolate peanut butter is a favorite as well."

"Ms. Levine, we both know you cannot afford to give away free cupcakes to anyone that stumbles in." Did he have an Eastern European accent?

"I am afraid I don't know what you are talking about. My business is, well, none of yours."

"What if I said I could help you triple your profits? Quadruple? Spin gold from this hay?"

"I would say I am not interested."

"Oh, but you should be."

Desperation seized Dana. "Let us say I am. What could you do?"

He smiled up at her. There was something predatory in that smile. One that sent chills of fright down her spine. "I see two obvious things right up front. First, your cupcakes are dry, while better than from a package not worth four dollars and fifty cents a piece. Please allow me to finish," she had opened her mouth to spew something most likely filthy and snapped it closed when he noticed. "Surely even you have noticed the decline in quality. Which leads me to my second point. You are doing it all on your own. It's too much for you to handle. The people walking down the street look in and you are in the back. They assume the business is not open and continue on."

She stared at him. She wanted to be angry, but he was right. On both points. She was frazzled and rushed. The care wasn't there. Just the need.

"I cannot afford a helper. I can barely afford to keep the lights on."

He nodded. "Then let's make a deal. I'll help for one week. In that week you will make enough to dig out of debt."

"And what do you get?"

He looked around the room at random. Then he looked at her and leered. She dreaded the words that would come next. And that she would consider them. He was an ugly little man. But desperate times call for disgusting measures.

"Your necklace will do as a fine payment."

Her hand reached up and clutched the broach. It had been a gift from her grandmother. She couldn't bear the idea of giving it away. But she heard the man from the bank in her head. She had three weeks to make three months of rent.

She nodded. "Fine. You have a deal, mister…?"

He smiled that shark-like smile again. "You may call me Grimm."

He extended his hand to her to shake and she recoiled at the over-long fingers. He seemed to not take notice of her act. She finally shook his hand and they both smiled cordially.

"When do you start?"

"Tomorrow. I'll be here at four to begin prep."

"I will see you then, Grimm."

He turned without a word and walked out the door and vanished into the throngs of people.

— — —

The next morning, she arrived at three thirty in the morning, like she always did. She had her headphones in and was singing along with George Michael as she danced around the kitchen setting out the butter to reach room temperature and getting the ingredients for the day's recipes. She went to the front and boxed up the day-old cupcakes and marked them down to half-price. Grimm's words came to her and she marked them down further. They really were not a good indicator of the store's quality.

She looked at her phone and saw it was four oh two. Maybe she had imagined the short man. Or his European sensibilities made him always fashionably late. She went back into the kitchen to get the ovens preheated and let out a squeal of surprise.

There stood Grimm on a milk crate, casually mixing ingredients into a bowl. The ovens were on and she realized she smelled something beyond delicious.

She popped out her headphones. "Good morning Grimm. What's that smell?"

He looked at her and nodded. "Good morning to you as well, Dana. It is a family recipe. Gingerbread cupcakes. I'm whipping up a cream cheese frosting. Do you have any raisins?"

"I am sure I do somewhere in storage. I don't do a gingerbread cupcake. The listing for the day is right in front of you."

"Today we shall add gingerbread to the list." He seemed as if it was only natural. "The scent will carry to the crowds, it will draw them in. Far better than orange or strawberry. Don't fret. We will still make your list. But the gingerbread shall be the star."

"This is still my business. Any changes should be brought to my attention before being decided upon."

The timer went off. What time had he gotten here? He jumped down from the crate and opened the oven door. The smell was truly delightful. Her mouth began watering and she cursed it as a traitor. He set the pan on the table to cool and finished making the frosting.

"The raisins?"

She made a sour face but went to get them from the shelf. She took a small satisfaction that they were on the top shelf. Feeling bad at her petty thoughts of him having to climb to reach them. She brought them out and set them on the table. He had one cupcake sitting, still steaming, with a dollop of frosting. He took a handful of raisins and set them with care on top. He held it out to her. She smiled as she saw he had made a smiling face in the frosting. She peeled the paper cup down and took a small bite. Then another. Soon she was looking in sadness at the empty paper cup and licking frosting off her lip.

"That is fucking amazeballs. Wow."

He nodded. "I will make them in small batches all day. Keep the front door open and it will draw in the visitors."

She wanted a second one. How long had it been since she ate even one? It reminded her of the gingerbread men from the small bakery back home.

"This is your secret weapon? The one that will quadruple sales?"

"It is indeed."

It was. At six the first customers roamed in. True to his word, the scent of the gingerbread called to the crowds. They barely kept up with the demand. As fast as he could bring her dozens of the different flavors they seemed to sell out. He never stopped cooking and she only went back to grab the fresh trays off the cooling racks. He looked unperturbed at the busy day. She felt exhausted by nine when at last the crowds began to thin.

It went like this each morning. He just seemed to be there when she turned around. Business was even better the second day as word of mouth spread. The third better than the second. Each day a new record for sales for the shop. On the fourth day the customers grabbed extra dozens for the weekend. No matter how frantic the rush, Grimm always had just enough cupcakes to fill the orders.

At the end of the fourth day as she flipped the sign from open to closed she went to kitchen.

"You were true to your word, Grimm. Better than in fact."

He nodded and continued his clean up.

"How about you stay on? We make a good team. We made enough that I sent two payments to the bank, even."

Before he could answer, her phone rang. "Dana Cakes. How may I help you?"

"Yes, I was hoping to place an order."

"I'm sorry but we are closed for the day. We open back up at six on Monday morning."

"That just won't do. My receptionist brought in your delicious cupcakes to the office. I've been raving all day about them. I need forty dozen on Sunday for an event I am holding."

"We usually require a couple weeks' notice for an order of that size."

"I understand. Truly I do. But this event is very important to me. And I think the publicity it would bring to your shop would be tremendous."

"Who is this? Is this a joke?"

"No ma'am. It most surely is not a joke. My name is Jeremiah Chaucer."

"The mayor? Very fucking funny. I'm hanging up now. This is not humorous in the slightest."

"Dana, may I call you Dana? I assure you I am serious. In fact, if you look out the window you'll see I am standing right outside hoping to talk with you."

She put the phone to her chest and saw him standing there like he did on television when he gave a speech on something or another.

"Fuck me running. It really is him."

He began laughing and she realized he had heard her exclamation. She rushed to the door and unlocked it.

"Pardon my language, sir. Please, come in."

He smiled and offered her his hand. It was a firm handshake. Not too firm as to crush, but reassuringly strong. The kind that was either a sign of confidence or a practiced skill. "It is fine. Believe me, I am only professional on camera."

And quite a bit more handsome in person. "That's a relief."

"Now about this order. It's for the Chamber of Commerce brunch. It is a pretty big deal that happens once a year. Your cupcakes will be the talk of the town. I'll pay double the price. Triple if you throw in a dozen of the strawberry for me."

"I don't know. Let me talk to my partner. Would you mind giving me a moment?"

"Not at all."

Dana's heart pounded as she tried to slowly walk into the kitchen. Grimm stood on his crate wiping off the table. She shut the kitchen door and stared at him.

"Did you hear that?"

"I did."

"So, what do you say? Partners?"

"No. We had a deal. I have still not been paid."

She looked at him in shock. "What do you mean?"

He pointed at the necklace. "I fulfilled my part. The necklace belongs to me."

"What about this weekend? I need your help."

"We had a deal."

She unclasped the necklace in a fit of rage and threw it at him. "Fine. Happy?"

He stuffed it into his pant pocket. "Content. Yes."

"So, about this weekend, are you willing to help me? I can pay you. Hell, this will put me ahead for a while. Even after ingredients. How much do you want?"

He gave her that smile again, the one that made her feel uneasy. He nodded as he decided. "I would like your ring."

"My ring?"

"Yes. That seems like a fair bargain."

"What the fuck is wrong with you? Are you always this creepy?"

"If this deal is unacceptable to you, I shall be on my way. Good luck this weekend. I have left the recipe for the gingerbread cupcakes in your binder. Hire yourself a helper to bake or run the register. I'll be off now."

He hopped down from the milk crate and took off his apron.

"Wait. Why *this* ring?"

"It is of significant value for services rendered."

"But not cash?"

He laughed, an evil little chuckle it seemed. "I have money. All that I could possibly want or need. No. I require more substantial payment for my talents."

She yanked off the ring and held it out to him. He simply raised his hands. "Take the fucking thing."

"No, that is not how a deal is made. We agree and shake. Payment after services have been rendered. I take it we have a deal?"

"You are seriously a creepy fuck, you know that? Yes, we have a fucking deal. You help me make the cupcakes and you can have my mother's class ring. It isn't worth a thing except for sentimentality. I don't see why you would want it."

They shook hands. It was like a band clasped around her head as they did. It was an odd feeling.

"The reason is mine and mine alone. I assume you want them as fresh as possible. Midnight tomorrow?"

She did the math in her head. That would cut it close, but they would be at optimal freshness to impress the business men and reporters. She nodded. "Midnight will be perfect. I'll gather the supplies we need."

"Fine. The mayor awaits."

She had nearly forgotten about him. She exited the kitchen and smiled at Jeremiah. "You have a deal sir. Plus, an extra dozen strawberry."

"That is fantastic! Wear something nice and join us. I'll have a van over at nine to pick them up. You can ride over with them and rub elbows with the snobs that really run things as my personal guest. Bring your partner as well if you want."

She made a face at the idea of Grimm coming along. "We will discuss it. Thank you for this, it is an honor."

"If they are as good as the one I had today, the honor is all mine."

Dana heard the kitchen door open and Grimm clear his throat. When she turned around there were a dozen assorted cupcakes in a box sitting on the counter. He was nowhere to be seen.

"And please take these with you. A little sample pack to try all we have to offer."

Jeremiah smiled at the offering. "I would be delighted. Thank you."

"My pleasure. I will see you on Sunday."

She stuck out her hand and Jeremiah brought it to his lips and gently brushed it. "I cannot wait."

— — —

"He says his name is Grimm."

She heard him breathe in disappointment through the phone. It was just the way he sighed. She imagined his lips pursed and his eyes, the only part of his face he could not hide his true feelings in, would have this sad look.

"And this, Grimm, he just stumbled in to help you out? Like a fairy godfather?"

She rolled her eyes. Thank God he didn't like video calls. "Yes. On Monday."

"And he wanted your necklace?"

"For fuck's sake. Yes. I told you. He said he could triple business in a week. All he asked for was my necklace."

"Could have been worse. He could have asked for your underwear."

"I don't know if that would have been worse or not. At least that is just pervy. The necklace felt, I don't know, intimate."

"You gave it to him?"

"We made a deal. I made more in four days than I have in the last three months. We barely could get them out of the oven before they were sold. It was like…"

"Like what?"

"Magic. Don't laugh. Don't you dare fucking laugh at me. I don't know how else to explain it."

This time he didn't bother hiding his sigh. "Well at least that is over. He's right though, you could use a helper."

"I really just sort of wish someone would come and offer to buy the store. It isn't what I thought. Sure as hell isn't what I want to do with my life. And it isn't over. Not yet."

"It isn't?"

"No. That's why I called. Guess who placed a huge order at closing yesterday?"

"Mary, Queen of Scots."

"Close. Try again."

"Connor MacLeod of the Clan MacLeod."

"Der can be only one. That's not it though."

"Scrooge McDuck?"

"What's up with all the Scottish bad guesses?"

"Fell asleep watching Braveheart. Who?"

"Jeremiah Chaucer."

"Shut the front door! Mister Mayor himself?"

"Mhmmm."

"Did he look as good in person as he does on television?"

"Better."

"I am so wet right now."

"Girl, me too."

"So, you decided to keep the Hunchback of Dana's Cakes on to fill the order?"

"He is amazing. Creepy as hell, but amazing."

"What did he ask for this time? He doesn't know about your hood piercing, does he?"

"Eww. No. My mother's class ring."

"He may be a demon. I don't like the vibes he is putting off."

"I think he is a lonely dwarf with too much time and too much money."

"If he is that loaded, send him my way. I need a sugar daddy and the right amount of zeros will make me do about anything."

"I don't think he goes that way. I'm not convinced he goes *any*way. He just bakes and smiles like a shark all day."

"The Eastern European accent leads me to believe he is into some freaky shit."

"Laying under a glass coffee table while you drop a deuce type?"

"One time! You'll never let me live that down."

"You never should have told me."

"It was the molly talking. Not me."

"Uh huh. Look, I've got to go. I need to pick out an outfit to wear."

"Where?"

"Jeremiah invited me to the Chamber of Commerce brunch."

"Ooooh. *Jeremiah* invited you."

"I could be first lady."

"The Mayor and his Cupcake Queen."

"Don't be jealous, Dixon. You're the only queen I know."

"Damn right. Wear that red dress. Your ass looks amazing in it."

"It does, doesn't it?"

"Not as good as mine would, but yes."

"I will call you tomorrow and let you know when I move into the Mayoral Palace."

"Just don't make any more deals with Grimm. You'll be asking me to help take out your labia ring and that is not happening."

"Deal. Talk to you tomorrow, Dixon. Kisses."

"Muah, Bitch!"

Dana hung up and stared into space. She couldn't get past the coincidence of Grimm and the sudden upturn in luck. She tapped the search bar on her phone and typed in Grimm. Pages of Grimm's Fairy Tales came up. She scrolled through them and remembered her mother reading them to her as a child. She added dwarf to the search. All that came up was Snow White hits. She didn't expect anything but still felt disappointed.

"Who the fuck *are* you?" She pulled a strand of hair to her mouth as she stared at the ceiling.

— — —

Dana awoke with a start. She hadn't meant to fall asleep.

"What the hell?"

She looked around the room and realized it wasn't hers at all. The room around her was dank and dark, the walls uneven stone. A threadbare rug covered the floor beneath her bare feet. She walked to the heavy wooden door and opened it up, grimacing at the squeak of the hinges. It opened into a long hallway lined with torches. The light mixed with heavy smoke gave the air a grimy feeling and she scrunched her nose at the stench.

"You are dreaming, dumbass. Nothing can hurt you."

She walked down the hall and tried each door she came upon, but they were all locked. Soon she found herself at a tower with a winding staircase that went both up and down. She chose down and counted the uneven steps as she walked down. At one hundred she reached a door and found it locked as well.

"Who locks all the doors in a dream?"

She made the climb back up, two hundred steps and she reached another door. She heard noise behind this door and hesitantly opened it. She froze in the threshold. Within sat a beautiful girl, no, a young woman sitting on a stool. She was singing a soft song in German. Dana let a gasp of shock as she saw another face, one she recognized, in the corner of the room.

It was Grimm. He was sitting on a low stool. His feet turning pedals on some strange wheeled device. His long-fingered hands feeding straw into the front of the device. Dana cleared her throat but neither heard her. She stepped in front of the singing woman and snapped her fingers. No reaction. She made faces. Stuck out her tongue, waggled her eyebrows, blew a raspberry right in her ear. Nothing. It was as if she didn't exist. She went over and examined the strange spinning wheel and let out a gasp of surprise. As Grimm fed handfuls of straw in, pure gold came flowing out the opposite end like fabric. She watched it pile up on the floor.

"What kind of dream is this? Is this my subconscious trying to tell me something? I know my cupcakes were dry, but I think straw is sort of going too far."

She jumped back as Grimm snapped his face towards her. He seemed to be staring right at her with a confused look on his face. Then he shrugged and went back to work.

"He is a creepy little bastard in my subconscious too."

"Who's there!" Grimm shouted.

She ducked involuntarily at the venom in his voice. Gone was the civility and calm he had shown. Now there was only anger.

"Who is where, kind sir?" the woman asked in alarm.

Grimm stared at Dana without seeing her. Then he let out an evil chuckle. "It is no one. I am jumping at shadows."

The woman looked frightened but nodded. Dana couldn't help but notice the way she seemed to constantly twist the ring on her finger as she watched Grimm spin straw into gold in front of her. A ringing sounded in the chamber. It grew louder and louder. Neither Grimm nor the woman seemed to hear it. Dana searched for it but there was nothing. And it kept growing louder…

She sat up in her bed. The ringing continued, and she laughed when she saw it was just her phone.

"Hello?"

"Dana. You said midnight. It is 12:01." Grimm's accented voice came into her ear.

She felt trepidation. She choked down the feeling. "I fell asleep. I can be there in fifteen minutes. I'm so sorry."

"It is fine. Fifteen minutes will not affect things. I shall be waiting for you." And then he hung up.

"What an odd fucking dude."

She hurried into the closet and grabbed the red dress. Dixon was right about how her ass looked in it. She smiled and threw make-up and heels in her backpack and ran out the door.

She arrived ten minutes later to find Grimm sitting patiently on the bench outside the shop. She gave a quick apology and opened the door as he hopped down. Once inside they got busy making the cupcakes. She put her headphones in and sang along as he used the mixer. As each pan came out of the oven she frosted them. Each in their own world, her singing and him baking.

It dawned on her after an hour or two how strikingly similar it was to her dream. She even found herself playing with her ring. Worrying it around her finger. Something on her face must have been off.

"Is something the matter?" Grimm looked at her intensely.

She gave nervous laugh. "No. I just had a strange dream and it came back to me suddenly."

He nodded as if this was perfectly normal. "Dreams can be portents of the future. Or so they used to say back home."

"Where is home?" She hated how her voice squeaked a little as she asked.

He cocked his head questioningly. "The Black Forest of Germany."

"I bet it's lovely there. A lot of castles back there?"

He nodded. "Not as many as there once were. But yes."

Dana couldn't shake the odd feeling about the dream. But she shook it off and kept working. And tried not to play with the ring on her finger.

— — —

The van arrived as she finished changing. She smiled at the driver as Grimm finished boxing the last dozen cupcakes. Dana smiled as she realized it was the strawberry specifically for Jeremiah himself.

"How do I look, Grimm? Okay for a fancy soiree?"

He looked her up and down appraisingly. "Yes. You look nice. Should fit right in, like a princess at a gala."

She blushed at the matter of fact way he said the words. "Thank you."

He looked at her patiently, expectantly. She cocked her head in confusion for a long moment.

"Oh. Yes. We had a deal, didn't we? This belongs to you. Fair payment for a job complete. I cannot thank you enough. In the span of a week I went from failing business owner to the chance of a lifetime. If you ever need a recommendation or get bored, I'm always here."

He accepted the ring and slipped it into his pocket. "If you are ever in need of my assistance, I shall be around. Thank you for honoring the deal struck. Good luck to you Dana. I have a feeling today will go very well for you. Perhaps better than you suspect. I must be off. Auf Wiedersehen, Fraulein."

She watched him leave as the driver loaded the cupcakes into the back of the van. The driver reached for the final box, but Dana grabbed them protectively. "These are for the mayor personally. I'll keep them."

The driver shrugged and shut the van door as she locked the shop. Her finger kept going back to the place where the ring had so recently rested.

"Goodbye Grimm. May our paths never cross again," Dana muttered under her breath as she got into the van.

— — —

The brunch went well. Amazingly so. Dana hobnobbed with the biggest and most influential business men and women in the city. All the while, the mayor, *please call me Jeremiah* stood by her side the entire time. It was electric being so close to him though Dana couldn't say why. She caught him looking at her as she spoke to the elite. When she felt out of her element he would touch her arm and she drew strength from that.

As the event was winding down she was showered with compliments on her baking prowess. Every single person raved about them. She was beside herself. This was the kind of publicity you could not buy. Reporters left cards in hopes of interviews. It was every bit of the dream she had on opening day finally come to fruition.

Soon it was Dana, Jeremiah and one last gentleman remaining as the staff hurried about on clean up. Dana was on that fine line of exhaustion and exhilaration as Jeremiah poured three glasses of scotch into crystal tumblers. The third member of the little gathering was named Gregor something. Too many consonants and not enough vowels made it impossible for her to even imagine pronouncing correctly. He was the owner of the local sports franchises, all four, though she could not have said what sport or named any of them. She laughed and explained her passions were more along the esoteric.

"I, too, never much cared for sports. My interests lie in money. So, I wish to make a proposal to you. In two weeks time there shall be a convention in celebration to the sports legacy of this great city."

"I don't see what that has to do with me."

"I am offering you the chance to be an official sponsor. Also, if you are interested, I would like to become a silent partner in your business. I can give you a storefront in each of the arenas and stadiums."

Dana's jaw dropped. "I don't know what to say. I am beyond honored. But there is no way I can do it. I don't have any employees. As of a week ago I was two months behind on rent!"

He nodded at her. "I am aware. I also see the potential in your offerings. Jeremiah gave you an impossible task in which you performed flawlessly. I offer you a second."

"Go on."

"Two hundred dozen. Next weekend. Fulfill this order and you will be flush with capital. Fail and you still have word of mouth and the Mayor behind you. Succeed and you will find yourself suddenly with five stores, with the potential to become a chain across the country. I know people, influential on a scale you cannot fathom, that will be more than happy to see you succeed."

"Why? Why me?"

"A feeling. Call it gut instinct. Call it intuition. I don't have any better answer than that."

Jeremiah smiled at Dana. "As of last Tuesday, your cupcakes went from a niche operation to an addiction. It is all we," he looked at Gregor, "have been able to think of. Before then, I had no interest in baked goods. Empty calories. Suddenly, you, my dear, have overtaken us all."

Gregor nodded. "I was with Jeremiah when his assistant brought in a box of the delightful little cakes. One bite was all it took to believe. What do you say? Take a chance on the chance of a lifetime?"

"And if I may be so bold as to sweeten the offer, once you have completed the order perhaps you would allow me the honor of dinner?" Jeremiah asked.

Dana took a big drink and coughed as it burned down her throat. "How can I say no to an offer like this." She smiled at Jeremiah. "Either of them? Consider me in."

Smiles around the table as they clinked glasses. Dana did her best to hold her anxiety in check. *How the fuck am I supposed to do this?*

Her smile faded as she realized she only had one option. Grimm.

— — —

Dana found herself back in the castle when she finally quieted her mind enough to sleep.

"Great. This fucking place again."

She opened the door and tried every other door again. She was not surprised to find them all locked. She stomped angrily down the corridor and took the stairs two at a time. This time she found the young woman sitting on the stool staring up at a regal man.

"If you can fill this room with gold by the end of the weekend, I shall make you my queen."

The woman leapt to her feet, a smile of pure joy on her face. "I shall rule by your side! Yes, your Majesty, it shall be as you ask. By the end of the weekend, this room shall teem with gold!"

The king smiled and ran a hand along her cheek. "Make it so, my love. We shall be the richest kingdom and live and love for the rest of our days."

The king left, and the woman spun about the room, her skirt twirling. Dana heard a voice behind her and turned in surprise to see Grimm standing in the room. She hadn't even heard the door open and close again.

The woman let out a happy laugh, ran over and hugged the evil looking little man. "I shall be queen! I require your assistance one more time."

Grimm nodded and rubbed his hands together greedily. "And what shall be our bargain this time? Surely a room filled with gold shall carry a high price."

The woman frowned. "I have nothing left to offer you, good sir."

Grimm cocked his head as if deep in thought. "I am sure there is something…"

Dana woke up before she could hear the new bargain. She looked about the room blearily before rolling over and falling blissfully, dreamlessly back into slumber.

When she finally woke for the day she only had hints of the dream, wisps floating in her mind. She made coffee and thumbed through her phone.

"Where the hell is it?" She scrolled to all her calls the day before. She knew she had talked to Grimm at 12:01. He had called her. Woke her up even. But there was no record of the call. She got online and checked her account, she remembered there were logs there as well. Her ex had been talking to another woman. He thought he was sneaky by always deleting the texts, but she was one step ahead. She found the woman's number this way and had begun her own chat history with her.

Nothing.

"How in the hell did he call me and leave no trace? Did I dream it? Am I really losing my shit at a time like this? Get your shit together, Dana. You cannot do this alone. You need the creepy bastard."

As if the universe heard her need, there was a knock on the door. She warily looked at the door for a long moment.

"Who is it?"

"Dixon, bitch, open up."

She laughed and got up and answered. He gave her a big hug and spun her around.

"So…"

"So… what?" she replied with a look of innocence.

"You know damn well *what*. Spill. How did he smell? Did you get to see the deputy mayor?" he winked, and she began laughing.

They sat and talked for hours about the events of the previous day. Giggling and going off on tangents about what she would do once she was a billionaire. Then she told him about the dreams. And the lost phone call.

"Like spinning straw into gold? Damn. That is a superpower I would love. I would look hot as hell wrapped in gold."

"You are so tacky. It was just a dream."

"But he *sort of* did that at the shop."

"My cupcakes are not like straw. They are an addiction, Jeremiah said so himself."

"Ooooh. *Jeremiah* said so. How are you going to get ahold of Grimm if you don't have his number?"

"I have no fucking clue. I was so relieved to be rid of him, I never even thought I would need his help again so quickly… Wait, you could help me."

"Sorry, I fly out first thing in the morning for Arizona."

"For what?"

"Drag review. We are doing a mini-tour slash vacay. Scottsdale, Phoenix and ending in Taos for a few days."

"Bail on it. Who needs another Judy Garland? I need you more."

"If I could I would, but Chris is out sick, and he is my backup. You need to find the creepazoid and quick."

Dana stared out the window and knew he was right. But how?

— — —

Dana got to the shop at four and began her prep for the day. She had done the calculations, if she ran the shop like normal and stayed until ten baking every night she would be able to possibly get it all done.

"I am so fucking screwed."

"Perhaps I can be of assistance."

She leapt back and brandished a knife against the intruder. It took a moment of pure panic to realize it was Grimm standing there.

"How in the fuck did you get in here?"

He smiled, that off-putting smile of his. "You left the door open."

"Why are you here?" She asked suspiciously. She needed to rein herself back if she was going to ask for his help, but she couldn't help herself. He was truly unnerving.

"I realized I made an error in the recipe for the gingerbread cupcakes. It would have proven to make them inedible. I was awake and wanted to correct it before it was too late."

"What error?"

"If you look, you will see I didn't put the right amount of molasses and too much salt. My calculations were off for the size of your batches."

She looked at the recipe and saw it was too much salt and half the amount of molasses. "A simple mistake. Thank you."

"I felt chagrined to say the least. Allow me to put down the correct amounts and I shall leave.

"Hold on…" she explained her predicament to him.

He nodded. "So, you would require my help a third time?"

"Very much so."

"Then a new bargain must be struck."

"What do you have in mind?" The echoes of the dream taunted her.

"This is significantly more than the previous times."

"I would make you a partner in the business."

"Again, I have little need for money."

"Then what?"

"Your first-born child."

Dana laughed at him. But then saw he was not smiling. She had always planned on never having children. But the idea of giving her baby to him was sickening. "You are being serious, aren't you?"

He nodded.

"That is the craziest, most fucked up thing anyone has ever said to me."

"So, you decline?"

"You are goddamned right I…"

Her phone rang. She looked down and saw it was Jeremiah.

"We will finish this in a second. Hello?"

"Dana, I apologize for the early call. I hope I didn't wake you?"

"Jeremiah! No, I was just going over the plans for the week."

"That is great! Gregor and I were talking about you last evening. He has every faith you will come through on your end. In fact, he asked me to reach out and tell you his previous order was too small compared to the expected turn out. He would like two hundred and fifty instead. Can you do that?"

She eyed Grimm as she freaked out in her mind. Promise her child to this monster or lose her chances at her dreams? If she never had a child, she really had nothing to lose. She was on the pill. And hadn't dated seriously for a year. Would she ever have the time to if she became a big time CEO? Probably not. What harm could a promise she never intended to fulfill cause?

"It won't be. Tell him he is on."

"That's fantastic! I knew you had it in you. I look forward to our dinner as well. I have reservations set up at Le Platypus, if you find that agreeable."

"The waiting list is two months long for there."

"Being mayor has its perks. I'm sorry to cut this short but if I don't jog now I'll never have time. We will talk again this weekend at the convention."

"Sounds great."

Jeremiah hung up and Dana turned to Grimm. "You have yourself a deal. Two hundred and fifty dozen cupcakes for my first-born child."

Grimm nodded and extended his hand. "A deal has been struck."

— — —

It went perfectly. They filled the entire order as the truck came to pick them up. Sure, it went to the wire, but where is the excitement in having an hour or two to spare?

Grimm left with a smile. Dana went to the convention and was overwhelmed. It was perfect. Gregor was true to his word. Within months she had five stores and a capable crew manning each of them. Within two years she had spread to three new cities. Three more and she was in fifteen. Soon she was running everything from an office in one of the many skyscrapers Gregor owned. She was a powerhouse. She had gone from nearly destitute to a success story out of a fairy tale.

And the date with Jeremiah? They had a great evening at Le Platypus. Then a second at opening night for the local baseball team where they snuggled up behind home plate. If the success of the business was quick and steady, the relationship was a whirlwind. The night she decided on expansion out of the city, Jeremiah proposed. One year later they married on the beach in Greece. Dixon was her maid of honor. He still swears he wore the bridesmaid dress better.

It was an ideal life. One that a million dreams could not hope to encompass. Dana was happier every single day. Sure, there were bumps, but she had love and a thriving business that managed to smooth them out.

She forgot about Grimm. On occasion she had a strange dream of waking in a castle, but they were like smoke when she woke. Life was too busy to be concerned about the past. If the errant thought of the strange little man ever crossed her mind she was hard pressed to say whether he had actually existed or not. Her autobiography (mostly ghost written) made no mention of three bargains. It talked of perseverance, rising up in the face of a challenge. Dixon and Jeremiah had never met Grimm. The man left no trace behind, no trail. He was like the dreams of the room where straw was spun to gold. Hazy and indistinct.

There was no way things could get better.

"Mrs. Chaucer? You have a call on line three," the voice through the intercom said.

"Who is it? I'm up to my eyelids in proposals for new locations in the Pacific Northwest. Have them leave a message."

"He says it is quite important, he says he is an old partner from the cupcake shop downtown."

"Gregor?"

"No ma'am. A *Grimes* I believe he said."

"Grimm?" Dana's blood froze in her veins.

"Yes ma'am Grimm. My apologies. He has an accent that was hard to understand."

"Tell him I am away from my desk and leave a number."

"Yes ma'am."

Dana turned and stared out the window. Grimm. He was real. Part of her felt relieved to know he hadn't been made up. Another part wondered what he could possibly want. They had no further business together.

Her cell phone rang. She looked at the display and relaxed when she saw it was Jeremiah.

"Hello dear."

"Ms. Levine." It was Grimm. She looked at her phone again and it no longer said Jeremiah. It showed no name, no number.

"How in the fuck did you get this number?"

"I have been well. Thank you for asking. I understand congratulations are in order."

"For what?"

"The end of bargain. You are with child. You still remember our deal, don't you? Two hundred and fifty dozen cupcakes for your first-born. I have waited patiently, but at last the time is upon us."

"You are insane. I am not pregnant. I just had a full physical yesterday morning. I'm on the pill. It's impossible."

"You may want to get this next call. Don't worry, I'll hold."

"Mrs. Chaucer?" the voice on the intercom spoke.

"What is it now?" she snapped. She felt bad.

"I am so sorry to interrupt, it is your doctor's office with the results of your physical."

"Put them through."

"Mrs. Chaucer, this is Carrie from Dr. Schmidt's office. We received the results of your blood work a few minutes ago and the doctor wished for me to call immediately."

"Okay. Is something wrong?"

"Quite the opposite. Congratulations, you are pregnant!"

"Oh fuck."

"Excuse me?"

"Sorry. Something came up here at work. Thank you. Have a great day. Good-bye." She hung up and stared at her cell and shakily brought it to her ear.

"In six months I shall come to collect my payment. Have a great day Ms. Levine." Grimm ended the call.

Dana sat staring at the phone. All color had drained from her face. Then suddenly she let a wail of anguish. Her receptionist came rushing into the room. The world grew fuzzy and Dana felt herself fall out of her chair. And then nothing.

— — —

She woke in the castle. Immediately she ran from the room and down the hall. She vaulted up the stairs and grabbed the wooden door. It was locked. It had never been locked before. She ran back to the hallway and checked each one down the row. Suddenly a new one swung in as she pushed. She nearly stumbled inside. There was the woman, now the queen, laying in bed with a newborn swaddled in her arms suckling on her breast. Dana yelled but the woman didn't hear her, couldn't hear her.

Then Grimm was there. "I am here to collect my payment."

The woman began sobbing and would not hand her child over.

Grimm smiled, and all his teeth had been filed to points. "You have three days. I'm nothing but fair."

"Three days for what?"

"Why, to guess my name. Get it right and you may keep your child. Get it wrong and the child is mine."

The woman screamed for help and two knights came into the room with swords drawn. Grimm just stared at them as the queen demanded he be slain. The first knight swung his sword and Grimm did not even move. He just opened his mouth, impossibly so, and snapped off the man's arm using only his teeth. A geyser of blood erupted from the stump. The second knight struck, and the sword bounced off Grimm's back. He turned with a grin and opened his mouth once more and stalked towards the knight.

— — —

Dana woke with a scream. She panicked as she didn't know where she was. Suddenly Jeremiah was in front of her, holding her hand and talking softly.

"You're okay. It's okay. You passed out. We are at the hospital." He bent in with tears in his eyes. "We are having a baby! The doctor thinks the surprise of the info is what made you pass out. I could not be happier!"

Dana smiled at him. But she didn't speak of Grimm. A part of her wasn't even sure it had happened at all. Jeremiah leaned in and kissed her lovingly, tears trailing down his cheeks.

She was released a few hours later. A few days went by and she watched her phone as if it were an adder. She took a leave of absence from work, it practically ran itself anyway and she had good people to make the decisions without her needing to oversee everything.

She had to tell someone, so she called the only person she could trust. And immediately regretted the decision.

"So, let me get this straight. You agreed to give a *dwarf* your baby for *cupcakes?*"

"That is not exactly all there was to it."

"But boiled down?"

"Yes."

"And now you're pregnant and the dwarf found you?"

"Yes."

"And he ate people in your dream?"

"Uh-huh."

"You, my dear, are fucked. He is some kind of Dracula."

"A vampire? You think he is a vampire?"

"He is immortal. He wants babies. It's the only answer."

"Dracula didn't want babies."

"I am pretty sure he did."

"He didn't. Not at all."

"Are you sure? Dracula, drinks blood, turns into a bat? Invades dreams. Has that claw hand?"

"Are you talking Freddy Krueger?"

"Shit. I think so. Bad acne? Ugly sweater?"

"You are no fucking help. I am serious. What do I do?"

"Guess his name? Girl, I don't know shit about movies. Unless it has The Rock in it. That Samoan can suck anything he wants on me."

"Thanks a lot, Dixon."

"Google that shit. I'll ask around, there is almost always one gay guy that knows the answer to any question."

"Thanks. Let me know if the gay hive mind has any answers."

"Will do."

— — —

She googled. She vaguely recalled doing this before and coming up with nothing. This time was no different. Just Grimm Brothers fairy tales. Something about that seemed right though. She dove into reading them. Eventually, after days, she had come up with nothing but a curiosity on how bad shit had been back in the olden days. It seemed kids were killed or killing things all the time. She ordered books online. They didn't hold any answers either.

She went to the library and found an old edition and took it to one of the big long tables and began thumbing through it. Halfway through she found something odd. The book went from page two hundred and three to two hundred and seven. She felt by the binding and found pages had been carefully cut out. She flipped to the table of contents, but it was missing as well.

"What the fuck?"

She took the book to the librarian and showed her the damage.

The librarian examined it carefully and clucked her tongue softly. "This happens sometimes. Especially with the old copies. It's a shame really. Back in the day if something was deemed offensive it was exited. Probably what happened here. I would imagine it had something to do with devil worship. That was a big no-no."

"Can I order a copy from another library?"

"Let me see. Yes. There are eight copies. I can get one for you in six to eight weeks. Which would you like?"

"All of them."

"That's an unusual request, Ms...?"

"Chaucer. Dana Chaucer, you probably know my husband."

The librarian's eye grew wide. She did in fact know who the mayor was. "I love your cupcakes. The gingerbread is my favorite."

"Thanks. I need them as soon as possible."

"I will call you when they arrive."

— — —

Weeks went by and her stomach grew larger along with her fears. She became moody and withdrawn to the point where the doctors insisted she remain off work. The stress was taking its toll on her. The baby was fine, a boy it turned out, but Dana was a wreck. She became obsessed with the fairy tales. At her five month point she received the call she had been waiting on.

"Ma'am, the books you ordered have come in. They will be available at the front desk."

She hurried and got dressed and ignored Jeremiah and his concerns. She raced to the library and had the librarian bring them to the table for her. She flipped through the first. No table of contents. She wasn't even sure there was one. She turned to the middle of the book, two-oh-three went right to two-oh-seven. The same with the next. All eight copies gave the exact same results.

She began sobbing in the middle of the library. Hysterically so. It got to the point where the librarian called City Hall and they got in touch with Jeremiah who came with a police escort to take his wife safely home.

Dana was broken. Hopeless. She sat in her room in a rocking chair staring outside at the trees and the flowers in the garden she had once so lovingly tended. She became despondent. Soon a full-time nurse was on duty to make sure she ate and moved around. It wasn't just Jeremiah that worried about her. Gregor had stopped by to check on her and she hadn't even acknowledged him.

One fall morning she sat in her chair staring outside when she saw something at the edge of the lawn. She stood and went to examine the strange shape. It was Grimm, the exact same as he had looked before, staring directly at her. He smiled that predatory smile at her and raised one too-long fingered hand to wave. She threw her chair at the window which shattered sending shards of glass and wood throughout the room. She was moved to a different bedroom afterwards. Jeremiah had special glass installed and over this he put black-out blinds that she could not control.

— — —

The baby came on time. When it was placed into her arms she seemed to snap back to her old self. Jeremiah was relieved to see his wife return to a semblance of normal after months of silence. She sang to the newborn and held it close to her breast to suckle. Jeremiah would not leave her side at the hospital. She looked over at him and felt the fear melt away from her. It was a nervous breakdown, the doctors said. An unconscious reaction to the pressures of becoming a mother. She never said a word about Grimm. Not to anyone. Only Dixon knew, and he was somewhere in Europe touring with the Drag Review. She was proud of him for following his dreams.

The baby was quiet. The room was quiet. The entire world felt at peace. She smiled for what felt like the third straight hour. The pain, a dull ache that the feeling of holding her child more than made up for.

"A bargain made, is bargain that must be paid."

The smile vanished off Dana's face. There in the doorway stood Grimm. "No. You may not have my child."

"But we made our deal in good faith, Ms. Levine."

"Then make me a new one. Take my life instead."

Grimm chuckled a cold mirthless laugh. "No. That is not the deal at all. How about a fair wager? Three days I shall give you in which to guess my name. If at sunset on the third you have not guessed it correctly, the baby is mine. And you and your husband's lives as well."

"Starting now of course."

And she began frantically guessing names. She grabbed the baby name book off the rolling table and read from A to M, nonstop. None of them were correct. Soon Jeremiah woke up and Grimm vanished as if he had never been there.

The next day he showed up again right before sunset. She read the rest if the book to no avail. Then she googled German names and began reading them. None of them were right. She could feel the melancholy desperation settle into her soul as she guessed over and over again. Eventually she grew exhausted and had read every name she could find. Grimm laughed and vanished again.

She didn't sleep. Just kept reading list after list of names. She wrote until she filled a notebook, carefully scratching out any she had tried. Jeremiah grew agitated and feared she was slipping back into her psychosis.

An hour before sunset on the third day, her phone rang.

"Hello?"

"Hey bitch, congrats on the shit and puke machine," Dixon said merrily.

Dana broke down into tears as she heard her friend's voice.

"That dwarf-fuck try and take your little monster?"

"He will kill Jeremiah and I at sunset today if I cannot guess his name. I've tried everything. I don't know what to do."

"Well guess who rode in on his magical unicorn with rainbow glitter and saved the day?"

"What are you talking about?"

"I am in Germany, all the sausage and beer I can take. It is gay heaven."

"How does that save the day? I'm going to fucking die. My baby is going to be stolen. Grimm is not human. I don't know what he is."

"A grimalkin."

"What?"

"Grimalkin. Some sort of fairy. Not the cool kind like me. Opposite side of the spectrum."

"How do you know this?" Dana demanded.

"Because I remembered our talk. Then you shut down on me and went all psycho staring out the window. There is place here called Grimmwelt Kassel. It is a museum to the Grimm Brothers. They are popular as shit over here. Like techno and wearing leather while being dragged around on a leash, popular. Like David Hasselhoff popular. Ninety-Nine Luft Balloons popular."

"Get to the fucking point. Life or death, Dixon, *my* fucking life."

"Fine. Way to ruin the story-telling. His name isn't Grimm. It is Rumpelstiltskin."

"Spell that for me please." She wrote it down on her pad of paper. "If this works you are my hero. We'll name him Dixon after his godfather."

"I am going to be his fairy godfather! Oh my goodness. I'll get him a little sequined dress and some cute little bondage wear!"

"Don't make me regret this."

"Too far? Yeah, I see that now."

"If I'm still alive, I'll call you tomorrow. I love you."

"Love to you guys as well. And I'm shaking my magical ass for good luck!"

"Thanks Dixon."

She hung up and waited for Grimm to arrive. He eventually did. Fifteen minutes before sunset.

"Give up, Ms. Levine?"

"No. I still have a list." And she began to read them with one eye on the sun outside. She went on and on until the last rays of the sun began to fade. Jeremiah walked into the room. And stopped in the doorway staring at Grimm.

"Honey, who is this?"

Grimm turned to him and smiled. His mouth began to stretch into a parody. A gaping maw filled with rows of sharp teeth. "I am your death, here to claim that which is rightfully mine!"

Dana smiled. "Honey, this is Rumpelstiltskin. My former partner at Dana Cakes."

Rumpelstiltskin let out a scream of rage and horror. He stomped his left leg so hard it sunk into the floor. He bellowed and fought to free his leg but only served to get himself stuck more and more. He writhed in agony and anger until his entire body sunk into the floor and the hole closed above him.

Jeremiah stood with a dark stain growing on the front of his trousers. He looked from Dana to the floor and back again. All Dana could do was laugh at it all. The relief and joy spreading through her. The nurse came in with the baby, Dixon, and stared in surprise at the mayor standing there with piss-stained pants. Dana's laughter rang throughout the hallways of the hospital like a ringing bell.

And they all lived happy ever after.

REVERBERATION

by Sam Kirk

When Annabelle came to, it took her a moment to figure out that her eyes were not failing her. It was just dark wherever she was. No matter how much she strained her eyes, she could not see a thing around her. Her hands were tied behind her and her lower extremities were bound to the chair's legs. Panic set in and she wanted to scream but couldn't. Her lips were taped shut.

Frantically, she tried to figure out where she was and how long she had been there. What she learned from all the books she had read and all the shows she had watched was that the longer the victim was gone, the harder it was for anyone to find them. Her chance of survival diminished with every hour she spent in captivity.

"What's the last thing that you remember?" Annabelle asked herself, trying to calm down her breathing.

But nothing came to mind.

"Think!" she screamed at herself.

However, the pounding headache made it impossible for her to recall anything beyond her sitting in a park.

Suddenly, the all-encompassing darkness started dissipating.

"Someone found me!" she thought to herself excitedly.

The bright light was blinding her now-accustomed-to-darkness eyes.

"Hello, sweetheart," said a chipper female voice coming from the direction of the light.

Annabelle started moving in her chair, trying to inch closer towards her savior.

"Calm down, sweetheart. It will all be over soon," the voice continued.

Finally, as the woman got closer, Annabelle's eyes adjusted to the light and they focused on the axe in the woman's hand. Her heart started beating faster, expecting the worst, but her reasonable mind tried to calm her down, explaining that the axe was to cut the rope with which she was tied.

"What is it, sweetheart?" the woman asked, noticing the girl's darting eyes.

"Oh, this?" she asked, lifting the axe.

"It's his birthday today, and I want to surprise him," the woman said and whacked Annabelle in the head with the butt of the axe.

--- --- ---

"Your father died." I heard my mom tell my dad the moment he stepped through the door after coming home from work.

"I didn't want to call you with that kind of news while you were driving," she said, putting her hand on his shoulder and following him out onto the back porch.

He did not utter a single word until the door closed behind them. Then, I presumed, he sat down and cried, processing the news.

Standing at the top of the stairs, I hesitated, not sure whether I should go down and console my father or go back to my room and give him some space. Mom had no idea I overheard her. Typically, after I come back from school, I play video games or chat with my friends while locked in my room until called to the kitchen for dinner. Tonight, as luck would have it, Joy had offered to come over and help me study for an upcoming biology test. Instinctively, I answered with a *Yes!* before I could even process what that meant.

Joy is the prettiest girl, and also the smartest one, in class. For years, I would get her a present even though I didn't draw her name for Secret Santa. She was then left confused as to why she received TWO gifts instead of one like everyone else. She has no idea I am her secret admirer, but that is alright. One day I will work up the courage and tell her how I feel. Now the stars have finally aligned, and they were shining upon me. The only obstacle was my parent's saying: "Our house, our rules," which meant that I had to ask permission whenever I wanted to invite someone over. I was on my way to ask Mom when Dad arrived from work.

Tonight's a no-go – I typed as soon as I sat back down in front of my computer.

? – Joy wrote in reply, rightfully confused.

I've been making googly eyes at her for forever, and now I was turning down her offer to come over and tutor me. I must be insane.

I just found out my grandpa died – I answered casually, hoping she'd understand.

OMG I'm so sorry – Joy typed back and finished it with an embarrassed smiley face, followed by a crying one.

I have to be there for my father – I continued, making sure that I left no doubt in Joy's mind.

There was nothing that would make me reject this tall, black-haired, hazel-eyed goddess — nothing beyond death.

Half an hour past the usual dinner time, after bidding my dream girl 'goodnight' and a couple of rounds on Counter-Strike, I began slowly descending the stairs again.

"Mom?" I called out.

"Dad?" I raised my voice as I got farther down the stairs, giving my parents plenty of time to compose themselves if they needed to.

The truth was I had no idea how to talk to my dad now that his father was gone. As a sixteen-year-old boy, this was my first close encounter with death.

"How do people grieve?" I wondered to myself.

"Oh, Charlie, I'm so sorry. I completely lost track of time and didn't realize how late it was," Mom apologized, as she walked into the kitchen.

"It's…" I started but quickly bit my tongue.

My first reaction was to say: 'It's alright,' but I knew that things were not. Mom didn't know that I knew, though, so I had to play it cool.

"Oh, honey, Grandpa Bill died," she said before I could decide on something neutral to say.

She crossed the distance between us with three large steps and hugged me tightly.

"How am I supposed to grieve?" I asked myself while awkwardly hugging my mother back.

"I'm so sorry, dear," she added while continuing to hold me and stroking my back.

"Why is everyone 'sorry'?" I wondered. *"It's not like either Joy or Mom killed Grandpa. They have nothing to be sorry for,"* I thought to myself, pondering the shortcomings of the English language.

"How's Dad?" I finally asked, trying to get out of her embrace.

Teenage boys aren't especially fond of maternal affection. At least this one wasn't witnessed by anyone else but the two of us.

"I think he's in shock," she answered as she let go.

She then walked up to the cupboard next to the fridge and pulled out a binder labeled *Take-out*.

"We'll order in today. Your pick," Mom said, handing me the blue folder filled with menus.

Pepperoni pizza was always an easy option, but I wondered if maybe I had a taste for something else this time around.

"Maybe Chinese?" I speculated, flipping through the menu pages.

"You don't have to go to school tomorrow if you don't want to," she announced.

Lifting my head from the binder, I looked at her quizzically.

"I know that with all the time you had spent together during summer vacation, you and Grandpa were close," she added, and I nodded slightly, going back to browsing the menus.

"General Tso's chicken," I decided.

"Okay, then. I will call in the order. You can go back to your room and play a little on your computer. It will take a while before the food gets here, so I'll call you when it arrives. But first, go outside and express your sympathies to your father," she said, picking up the phone.

— — —

"Hey, Dad," I said, as I stepped out onto the porch, automatically feeling stupid, not knowing what to say.

He was sitting in his usual chair and didn't even look at me when I spoke.

"I'm sorry about Grandpa," I continued, realizing that I used the same silly phrase that Mom and Joy did.

Out of ideas, I placed my hands in my pockets and just stood there for a moment. Dad nodded slightly but didn't say a word. He just kept staring into the distance.

"In shock indeed," I thought to myself, remembering what Mom said in the kitchen.

"Mom's ordering Chinese," I said, hoping that would snap him out of his trance.

But he didn't say a thing and the silence quickly became uncomfortable. Since I had no idea what else to say, I took an audible breath in and then went back inside the house.

"Maybe I should ask Joy to come over anyway?" I wondered, having seen my out-of-it father.

"How's your father?" Mom asked as I began ascending the stairs.

"Huh?" I asked, lost in thoughts of Joy.

"Your father. How is he? Did he say anything to you?" Mom repeated.

"No. Dad didn't say a word," I answered and went on to climb the stairs.

Her loud sigh led me to believe that he did not utter a single word to her, either.

Once in my room, I laid down on my bed and took a deep breath, finally taking in the news of Grandpa's passing. It's been a while since I thought about Grandpa. Summer, three years ago, came to mind. It was my first vacation with Grandma and Grandpa. My father moved away when he was 19, but then three years ago, work brought him back to Montana. So off I went to spend the summer with my grandparents, whom I had not seen for years.

At first, things were going well, and I enjoyed helping out on the farm with all the crops and animals. But after a few weeks, the routine became too mundane. The city boy in me started protesting against waking up at the crack of dawn to feed the cows, the chickens, the pigs, and the sheep. That, combined with milking the cows, quickly started taking a toll on me. Whenever I could, I would lay down underneath a big apple tree and try to figure out what to do to keep myself away from all the chores. Since the farm was somewhat isolated, I had no neighbors my age with whom I could play. We did not have neighbors at all.

My luck turned around one day when Grandpa asked me to go into town with him. He needed to get some parts for his tractor, so off we went. Driving through the countryside with the windows down was the most exciting thing I had done in a while. When we entered the enormous outdoor market in the nearby town, I was in awe of how something like this could exist only a couple of miles away from the farm. All of the hustle and bustle was like music to my ears after only hearing the noises farm animals make for what seemed like ages.

That day, I met the girl of my dreams. Her long, blond hair bounced from left to right and from right to left as she walked. Her daisy dukes made her already long legs seem endless. I had no idea one could fall in love so quickly, never even having spoken to the other person. But before I could do anything about it, she walked away from the tomato stand and disappeared into the crowd.

Hoping that I could find her somewhere along those hundreds of paths of this market, among thousands of people, I convinced Grandpa to get a beer at the local tavern while I went to search for the items from Grandma's list.

The blistering heat was getting to me, so I stepped inside a supermarket by the market's main artery. Suddenly, I scored gold. The love of my life was only a few feet away from me. Trying to keep my eyes glued onto the back of her head, I kept tossing random items into my shopping basket. One of them must not have made it in because I tripped and fell flat on my face.

"Ahhhh," I murmured, picking myself up and inspecting my nose for fractures.

"You alright?" asked the angel standing above me with an extended hand.

The object of my affection was even more beautiful up close.

"I just… The floor must be wet or something," I answered, grabbing her hand to steady myself as I got up.

"Or something!" she said and chuckled, placing a bottle of shampoo in my basket.

"How many fingers do you see?" my savior asked, holding two of them up.

She looked like she was a few years older, with her breasts already nicely shaped.

"You're human. You have five fingers on each of your hands," I answered smugly.

"I'm Annabelle," she said with a warm smile and lowered her hand.

Her turquoise earrings matched her eyes.

"Charlie." I introduced myself, marveling at her beauty and my luck. "Would you like to go get some ice cream?" I asked, still red with embarrassment.

There was no way she was interested in such a klutzy person like me. She looked at her watch and I exhaled. It's not like I didn't see that coming. And, in a way, I was glad she refused. I had no idea what I even thought when I asked her out.

"What would we even talk about?" I admonished myself, realizing that my fall would provide only so much comedic relief.

"I have a piano lesson at 2, so we only have about an hour, but sure. Why not?"

"It's alright. I understand. Wait; what?" I asked, blinking rapidly in disbelief.

"Yes, I would love to get some ice cream with you," she said, flicking her hair coquettishly and then grabbed my hand, pulling me towards the exit.

The shopping basket filled with random items was left haphazardly on a nearby shelf.

My nerves were off the charts. I had no idea what I was doing or how to proceed. Luckily, the ice cream shop was nearby, and so small talk about the weather was sufficient. We each ordered two scoops. I went with chocolate and pistachio, and Annabelle asked for strawberry and vanilla.

"Would you like to go and sit down by the pond?" I asked between licks, trying to fill in the awkward silence.

There was a small park on the other side of the ice cream shop, which I thought would be perfect for us to sit down and consume our desserts. Walking down market paths filled with people on a sweltering day didn't seem romantic at all.

"There's a bench underneath a tree on the other side of the park. Let's go there" she answered decisively.

Another quality that I liked about her - she was not afraid to take charge. She made me feel as if I had a chance, and she was going to make a man out of this boy.

We crossed the street and walked to the bench without uttering a single word.

"Are you always this quiet?" Annabelle asked after a while.

"I've never done this before," I answered, embarrassed.

"Never done THIS? What? Sit on the bench? Or eat ice cream? Or both?" she asked with a straight face.

"A girl with a good sense of humor. Jackpot!" I thought to myself.

"I've never been on a date," I answered after swallowing what felt like a golf ball.

"Oh, you think this is a date?" she asked and looked me deep in the eyes.

I wanted to put my foot in my mouth. This whole situation was painful to watch, and I knew it.

"Ummm…" I started but had no idea how to finish this without digging myself in deeper and losing whatever shred of dignity I had left.

"Relax. I'm just pulling your leg. You're cute, and I'd like to get to know you better," Annabelle said, slightly blushing and batting her lashes.

She then leaned in closer and placed her hand on my leg. I was so out of my depth. Her lips were now inches away from my ear.

"Someone's watching," she whispered.

Her words were like a cold shower, and I quickly turned around.

"Grandpa!" I said with irritation.

"There you are. I've been looking all over for you," Grandpa said, coming closer.

"I had a little accident at the store and Annabelle helped me out, so I thought I'd repay her and at least take her out for ice cream," I explained, hoping that he would get the hint and leave.

"Stop horsing around and get up. We gotta get back home," Grandpa replied without even acknowledging Annabelle.

She was stunned, and so was I.

"Chop, chop!" he said before turning around and walking back towards the street.

"Give me your hand," I asked her, pulling out a pen from my pocket.

"Here's my number," I said, writing ten digits on the palm of her hand.

I looked into her eyes one more time. She nodded her head slightly as if to let me know that she would call me soon.

But I never heard from her again.

"Who was that whore?" Grandpa asked when we got to the car.

"EXCUSE me?" I asked, wondering if my hearing was impaired due to the fall.

"That blonde hooker in the park," he answered without skipping a beat.

That was the first time I ever heard him swear. Taken aback by this revelation, I could not think of a proper reply.

"I think it's best you go back home tomorrow," he said, before turning on the radio and maxing out the volume.

Not another word was uttered as we drove.

"Don't upset Grandma," he said as we approached the house.

No matter how much I tried, he ignored all my questions regarding Annabelle for the rest of the day.

The next day he drove me to the train station and didn't even get out of his truck once we arrived.

"Grandpa, what's going on?" I asked, hoping that he would respond this time.

"I don't want you fraternizing with the lowest of scum. One day you will understand. Now go back to where you came from."

Tired of not getting any answers, I got out of the car and walked onto platform number four.

Within three hours, I was home.

"Was it THAT bad?" Mom asked me as I got off the train.

I stared at her and Dad blankly, not knowing what Grandpa had told them.

"Grandpa said you just couldn't take that lifestyle anymore and that you wanted to come back home," she continued.

I must have subconsciously nodded because Mom stopped prodding and she just hugged me tightly.

Once at the car, I put my headphones on and lost myself in the music. There were no answers to be had. My head was already hurting from trying to figure out why Grandpa was so hostile towards Annabelle and why he sent me home. What I found peculiar was my dad looking at me periodically in the rearview mirror the whole way home.

"Is everything alright, son?" he finally asked when we arrived at home.

"Everything's fine. I couldn't take the roosters crowing at five am every day," I answered dismissively.

The rest of the summer was unremarkable.

— — —

"Charlie, the food is here," Mom shouted from downstairs.

"Coming!" I yelled as I got up from the bed.

"I thought we could maybe all sit down and talk, or even watch a movie as a family. You know, be together during such a difficult time. But your father refuses to come into the house or even speak to me," Mom said visibly perturbed.

"Would you like some company?" she added.

"I think he needs you more," I answered, already turning back for the stairs.

She sighed loudly and slumped in the chair.

Upstairs, I took a bite out of my meal, and my stomach rumbled angrily. It must have been hungry, so I took another forkful. This time it felt like my stomach started performing summersaults.

"What the heck?" I wondered, leaning in closer to smell the food.

Everything seemed perfectly fine with my General Tso's chicken, but something was very wrong. The onset of nausea made me leave my food on my desk and run to the bathroom.

With my heart racing and my difficulty breathing, my chest felt as if it was getting impaled. Once in the bathroom, I slid down, with the help of the wall, onto the floor. The world in front of me started spinning. I could not feel my hands. I was hot one second and cold the next.

"Mom?" I called out but knew that I wasn't loud enough for her to hear me.

It was official – I was dying. On the bathroom floor. Alone. But I didn't want to go down without a fight, so I pulled myself up to my feet and leaned against the sink. The freezing-cold water felt like knives on my face but that made the other symptoms vanish for a moment. I took a deep breath and turned off the faucet. My heart started beating out of my chest again. My fingers started tingling.

"What is going on?" I wondered, feeling scared one second and angry the next.

Splashing my face with ice-cold water again helped, so I kept doing it for a little while longer until I could go on for a full minute without the mysterious symptoms. A quick search on my phone helped enlighten me as to what was happening. I had a panic attack.

"But why?" I asked myself.

— — —

Even though I did not want to spend the next summer at the farm, my parents still sent me there, reassuring me that the rooster was long dead.

"Grandma made broth out of him," Mom said before I got on the train.

I had no idea what to expect.

"Hey there, Sport," Grandpa greeted me at the platform as if nothing happened.

It took me a while to recalibrate myself, but I cleared my throat and slapped a smile onto my face in the end.

The whole way from the train station to the farm, Grandpa made small talk. He asked me about school and sports, to which I replied with short, meaningless answers.

"Got a girlfriend?" he finally asked as we approached the house.

"No," I replied embarrassingly.

"*Good.*" I could have sworn that was what he said.

"Why is that?" I asked, hoping for an answer that would explain what happened the previous summer.

"Why is what?" he asked, opening the door to the house.

"You said it was good that I didn't have a girlfriend. Why is that?" I spelled it out for him.

"I didn't say that," he said, and before I could say anything else, I heard Grandma coming towards us.

"Charlie! I just pulled some chocolate chip cookies out of the oven," she said, grabbing me by the hand and leading me towards the kitchen, leaving Grandpa behind.

The next couple of days were uneventful. My grandparents allowed me to sleep in and only asked that I help them pick the strawberries. Grandpa acted like nothing happened last summer and I decided to let things go. A clean slate. A fresh start.

"Want to go for a walk?" Grandpa asked one evening.

"Sure, but isn't it too late?" I wondered audibly, looking out the window.

"Not now. Tomorrow morning. Mushroom picking," Grandpa replied.

"Yeah, sure," I answered earnestly.

He woke me up at the crack of dawn the next day.

"Here we go again," I thought to myself, wondering if we were going to go back to me getting up with the chickens and performing all the chores daily, like last year.

The dew glistened on the grass. The sun was barely coming out from behind the horizon.

"Go to the shed and get us some baskets. I have a feeling we will find a lot of mushrooms today," Grandpa said as we exited the house.

The shed was dark and frankly slightly creepy. All the farm tools were stored here. Spider webs were everywhere, and mice were running from one corner of the room to the other. However, just like Grandpa said, the baskets were on the right-hand corner near the entrance, so I grabbed two of them and turned around towards the exit. After a moment of hesitation,

I turned right back around and grabbed one more basket just in case.

We filled all three of the baskets before we knew it.

"Time to go back. Well done. Grandma will be waiting with a nice breakfast," Grandpa said and turned towards the direction from which we came.

Or so I hoped. All I could do was trust Grandpa since my sense of direction was lost five minutes after we entered the forest. I breathed out a sigh of relief when we came out of the woods, and I saw the farmhouse in the distance.

"We'll take the smallest basket in for Grandma. She might make dinner with these beautiful mushrooms. But the rest, we have to dry out, so they don't go bad too quickly. There is a drying rack in the shed. Can you carry those inside and spread the mushrooms on the shelf?" Grandpa asked.

"Sure," I answered, grabbing the other basket out of his hand.

The two baskets were rather heavy, and so I waddled into the shed, stopping every couple of feet. As I approached the shelf, I heard footsteps only a few feet behind me. Normally, that wouldn't scare me, but any noise in a dark shed filled with vermin can make the hairs on the back of your neck stand on its ends.

"Ah, it's you!" I said gladly, seeing Grandpa standing in the door.

"Yes, it's me," he said as he closed the door behind him.

"I decided to come and help you with the mushrooms," he added.

"Is there a light in here?" I asked, feeling silly that I did not spot it sooner.

"No need for the light. I know what I'm doing," Grandpa replied and moved towards me.

"This must be some hillbilly trick to heighten your senses." I thought to myself.

I nearly jumped when he placed his hand on my shoulder.

"There you are," he said, before dragging his hand lower towards my crotch.

"Grandpa, what are you doing?!" I asked, jumping backward and hitting the shelf.

"Be still now. It will be easier that way," he said quietly as if he was looking out for me.

— — —

"I wanna come home," I told Mom on the phone the next day.

"Why?" she asked.

"Because. I don't want to be here anymore," I answered, peering at Grandpa who was sitting in the corner.

"Charlie, do you want to be a man?" she asked out of the blue.

"What?" I didn't know where this line of questioning was heading.

"You won't become one sitting at home all the time playing video games. You have to GROW UP. Grandpa will show you how," she replied.

If only she knew what was going on around here. If she only knew that Grandpa had already turned me into a man. A man who would go on to having panic attacks at the mere recollection of him. I felt a little more broken every time Grandpa and I met in the shed. But there was nothing I could do. He was stronger than me. I was a kid and he was the adult. No one was going to believe me. Plus, I was convinced that I must have done something to provoke him.

Last summer, I was able to land a job at a scout's camp, so I was able to finagle my way out of going to the farm. This year, with summer approaching, I was getting nervous about coming up with an excuse for why I shouldn't spend some time with my grandparents. But Grandpa died. Just in time. Thankfully. I didn't have to worry anymore. The devil went back to hell and I was finally free. Telling my parents that I was happy about Grandpa's passing would raise a couple of red flags, so I chose not to say anything and pretend to grieve. But the problem was that I didn't know how to do just that. Fortunately, Mom blamed my awkwardness on my young age and my inexperience in mourning. Admittedly, I had no idea how to lament my grandfather.

— — —

I wore dark sunglasses to the funeral, just like everyone else. Only they were wearing them to hide actual tears. I did that only to blend in and not look like a psychopath. The wake was held in a town not too far away from my grandparents' farm. A handful of people showed up, mainly my father's co-workers to show support in time of need. After the official gathering, Grandma invited us over to the farm. I didn't want to go, but she insisted, and everyone was worried that she would collapse or go insane if she didn't have family support at such a difficult for her time.

"Hello, Mother," said a blind woman, entering the kitchen.

"Sally!" Grandma said, unable to hide her surprise.

She got up and ran towards the door to greet the new arrival.

"Who's that?" I asked my father quietly.

"That's your Aunt Sally," he answered calmly.

"Aunt?" I thought to myself, never having met or heard about her.

The two women embraced awkwardly as if they barely knew each other.

"You all catch up and I'll go outside and start a fire," Grandma said and rushed outside.

It turns out that Auntie moved away from home even before Dad did and lived in Texas for the past twenty-some years.

"Hi, Sally," Dad said with a hint of nostalgia in his voice and got up to hug her.

Unlike the hug between her and Grandma, this one was filled with deep emotions. I think I even saw a tear in Dad's eye and one roll down Auntie's cheek. We spent a few minutes catching up, mainly talking about me – how old I was, who I looked like, and what kind of a child I was.

"Let's go outside and check up on Grandma," Mom said and ushered us out the door.

The fire was burning high by the time we got to the fire pit.

"Sit. Sit down," said Grandma, pointing to the logs spread around the fire.

"How could I forget? You all must be starving. Let me go get some food," she added.

"It's alright. I'll go. What do you want me to bring out?" Mom asked her, already walking towards the house.

"No, no. Sit. I need a minute. Bond. You haven't seen each other in ages. And did Charlie even know he had an aunt?" she asked but left without waiting for an answer.

Grandma walked away towards the house and Mom came back to sit down next to me. With Dad to my left, Mom to my right, and Aunt Sally next to Dad, we spent most of the time somberly looking into the fire.

"Okay, I'm back. I brought you all a meat pie. Homemade. Naturally." Grandma said and passed one to each of us with a warm smile.

"I think it's high time we talked," she added once she sat down.

"Your father…father-in-law…grandpa died," she started. "And so today I would like to honor his memory by coming together and talking about him. Sharing our memories of him."

Only the crackling fire was heard in the air.

"I'll go first," Mom began. "I did not know Bill all that much. Actually, not at all. We always lived far away, promising one another that we would visit soon. Soon never came. And I feel awful for that. I only saw him at our wedding. But even then, we didn't spend much time together. Me, being the bride, I had so many guests to entertain…"

My blood was boiling. This man tortured me and scarred me for life and now I was supposed to talk about how great of a person he was? But I couldn't just say he was a monster. Not today. Not ever. He was dead, and it was a low blow to speak badly about someone unable to defend themselves. Plus, I did not want my father to lose the illusion of his father being perfect. I couldn't be selfish. I HAD to keep quiet.

"You didn't see him much because I wouldn't let you," my father interrupted.

My mother paused and looked at my dad, quizzically.

"I'm sorry you guys, but I can't do this," he added and buried his face in his hands.

"What?" Mom asked, without a clue as to what Dad was trying to say.

But I knew. I could feel my father's anger. His shame. His fear. His disgust. I could sense all that because all of those very same emotions were bubbling inside of me.

"He molested me," he said so quietly that I thought no one but me heard.

Mom gasped, which meant she heard what he said.

"For years. That's why I left home," he said, lifting his head from his hands.

"Dad?" I said, turning towards him.

"What, son?" he asked, but he knew the answer before I even opened my mouth.

"Oh, no, no, nooooooooooo!" he shouted and threw himself onto the ground.

"Charlie?" Mom looked at me.

Her eyes were begging me to deny what she thought she heard. But I couldn't. I just stared blankly at her and so she proceeded to sob.

"Well, this is a great family reunion. I thought I was the only victim here," Aunt Sally said, and all eyes darted towards her. "I did not lose my vision because I looked at the solar eclipse without a welding mask. I lost it because Dad rubbed chemicals into my eyes. On purpose.

"I saw what he did to you, Jim. I walked in on you two in the shed one day," she continued.

"He could not risk me telling anyone about what I saw so he chemically castrated my eyes and forced me to move out, threatening to tell everyone I was sleeping around. I didn't want to leave you with him, but he gave me no choice."

Once finished, she stood up and used her white cane to carefully approach Dad.

"I'm so sorry I failed you," Aunt Sally apologized, lowering herself to the ground.

They embraced and sobbed together in union.

"Enough of this crap!" Grandma roared.

"I cannot stand your whining any longer. Yes, you're blind, but you are a famous sculptor, Sally. Would you be where you are now without your dad blinding you?" she asked and paused.

All eyes were finally on her, blinking in disbelief.

"Oh, Boy, he touched your privates. Well, maybe that cured you from being a homo. I was anxious about you when you were growing up, Jim. And look at you now: a wife and a kid. Well done," she continued.

"And you..." she turned towards me and pointed her finger. "You are too young to be getting girls pregnant. He had to do SOMETHING to keep you at bay."

"Pregnant?" I was confused.

"Yes, that's how it starts. You meet, you chat, you flirt, and before you know it, you have a kid on the way, and your whole future is ruined!" Grandma explained.

"I'm sorry you didn't get the chance to get to know Bill," she said, turning to my mother. "Who knows how he would have enriched your life?"

"He was a gift to you all. I am the real victim here!" she snarled, sitting back down.

"How's the pie?" she asked, shoving a forkful of the meal into her mouth as if nothing happened.

"Eat!" she shouted with her mouth half full.

No one had ever seen Grandma angry. Everyone was stunned and scared so we each obeyed and placed another bite in our mouths.

"Esther, you're scaring us," Mom voiced her concern.

"Oh, boo-fucking-hoo," Grandma hissed. "Would you like to know what he did to ME?" she asked bitterly.

"I've carried this burden for way too many years. Do you know how we met? No? Well, let me tell you," she said and repositioned herself on the log. "He was a handsome stud," she said with a smile.

"He always had girls throwing themselves at him, fresh for the picking. I knew I stood no chance with my plain looks and quiet demeanor, so I watched him from afar, hoping that maybe one day he would see less value in them and more value in me," Grandma said, and her face hardened.

"I remember as if it was yesterday: he was eighteen; I, barely sixteen. I followed him deep into the woods one day because I wanted to see what he was going to hunt. One moment he was entering a wooden shed and the next I heard a gunshot. Fearing for his life, I ran inside.

"'Who are you and what are you doing here?' Bill asked me, but I could not speak, too distracted by the blood on the cheerleader's costume.

"So much blood.

"'I've seen you around quite a bit. Are you following me? Wait, are you IN LOVE with me?!' he asked, and all I could do was nod.

"We became so close that day. He explained to me that pretty girls disgusted him, and I beamed with joy. He confided in me that he liked punishing them by killing them. We hung out for a couple of months and occasionally I would help him lure them out into the shed in hopes that he would like me more. It must have worked because before I knew it, we conceived Sally and were getting married.

"'Are you okay with all this?' he asked before the ceremony.

"I was so in love with him that I couldn't imagine NOT marrying him. I was so close to getting what I wanted. I knew full well that no one else would look at me twice.

"'Of course,' I answered.

"'Alright, then. We are in this together now,' Bill said as we became man and wife.

"The more we killed, the more we craved. I was the brain behind the operation – always trying to find a new victim — a new way to catch them and make them pay. I also took care of the disposal in a creative way, so no one would track the killings back to us," she finished with a proud smile.

"How?" Dad asked, his voice trembling.

"Patience. We'll get to that in a moment." Grandma dismissed him with a wave. "I wanted to honor them," she said gleefully.

"Unlike Bill, I had some positive feelings towards all these pretty girls. I was grateful for them since it was because of them that he looked at me and saw me as someone worthy of his attention. We slowed down after a while and moved out here to limit his temptations. And then Charlie showed up," she paused and looked at me.

My eyes widened.

"Annabelle," I muttered.

Grandma's earlier remark finally made sense.

"Yes, her. I couldn't let her destroy you," Grandma said with conviction. "But don't worry. I honored her, too. Bill was very impressed with my birthday meat pie, not having had one in a few years.

"He was the most handsome man I've ever seen. Gay or not, child molester or not, he never laid a finger on me. I could blame myself for becoming a killer and a monster, but I did it all for him, hoping for a reward one day. But that reward never came. In the end, I was just another tool in his toolbox," she said with a sad face.

"So, to honor his memory, I turned him into his favorite thing: a meat pie," she announced with excitement.

We all looked at the half-eaten meals in front of us and then at one another.

"Excuse me for a moment. I need to use the bathroom," Grandma said before standing up and walking away, leaving us all speechless.

We didn't know whether she was serious or not. Surely, we didn't just eat Grandpa.

A few minutes later, a loud bang pierced the silent night and we all rushed towards the shed — even Aunt Sally, who was helped by Mom. Grandma laid in the middle of the shed. The mushrooms drying on the shelf behind her now painted red.

THE GUEST HOUSE

by Chris Nelson

Room One

Duncan's dream had been the same each night since he had first booked in to the small seaside guest house nearly two weeks earlier. He woke every morning at around eight-thirty with the image still swimming around his head as if it were afraid to let him leave and stumble into another day. The picture was as clear as anything that he might have seen the previous day, or the day before that, except for the fact that it wasn't. It wasn't his mind recalling events or restructuring facts; it wasn't conjuring a vision or a particular fantasy, nor was it his subconscious playing idly with images that he had seen or imagined from books. His dream came at some point when he was asleep and hung around until the moment that he awoke and then thrust itself in front of him. Or had it only just formed itself in the moments immediately before his body began to stir to the rhythms of a new day? Duncan was unsure, but of one thing he was certain - the dream remained the same.

To say that it was a dream was perhaps affording it rather more significance than it deserved however. When Duncan first started to emerge from his slumber, when his brain began to acknowledge the sounds that emanated from somewhere outside of himself, and his eyes began to accept the light that had invaded his room, the scene inside his head was as vivid as any reality, and yet that was all it was - a scene. For ten consecutive nights he had awoken to the same scene and yet was unaware of what had happened prior to that point in his dream. Of course he had tried to imagine the events which might have led to the scene that replayed behind his eyes; he had daydreamed fantasies and build entire scripts around it, but as the morning light made itself fully known to him, he had always realized that these dramas were not his dream, and, as a result, left him disappointed and cold. Try as he might, Duncan was unable to drag himself back into his dream, even though it revisited him each night, to see what was hidden from him. All that ever remained was the fleeting image weaving itself in and out of his consciousness until it slipped away quietly like a fishing boat into the fog.

He was laying face down on the bed, the woman's thighs, full and as smooth as satin, spread on either side of his head. Her knees were bent up, or at least he assumed that they were, and he was aware of the creamy texture of her flesh, so close to his face. His arms stretched out from his shoulders, but seemed to disappear before forming hands, his awareness of the feel of her skin reaching him in subconscious waves. He knew that he was kissing her and also that she was drawing pleasure from his movements. He tried to raise his head, to lift his eyes, straining in desperation to gaze across her belly, the form of her breasts and to see her face, but each attempt proved fruitless. As pleasurable to her as his actions were, however, Duncan, with each passing night, was finding less gratification and greater frustration in his dream. Each morning, as his eyes forced themselves open, flickering momentarily against the light, Duncan found himself more and more consumed by one passion, one desire: to discover the identity of the woman who had hijacked his dreams.

Room Two

Margot Henderson sat at the small, Formica-topped table in one of the two simple but functional chairs and gazed out over the roof-tops at the distant mountains. Hers was the only room that didn't afford its occupant a view of the sea, its window opening out over the rest of the small town which seemed to stretch like tree roots to the foothills beyond. When Margot had taken the room - the last one available - Claudette Mason, the proprietor of the guest house, had explained, in almost apologetic terms, that although the view of the mountains was spectacular (which it was), it was sadly not of the sea. Margot had replied that she did not mind, and that the room would be perfect for her; besides, the sea was no more than a five-minute walk from the house and simply being here was enough to satisfy her need for a change of scene.

What Margot did not tell Claudette, though, was the real reason for her taking a room in the guest house. This was not due to any embarrassment or sense of shame on her part, but rather that her story was, in her eyes, merely far too stereotypical these days: a middle-aged woman whose children had grown up, forged lives for themselves and left the family home, and whose husband had then abandoned her for the obligatory younger woman. A messy and acrimonious divorce followed after which Margot had felt that she wanted to leave all that she had known behind her, even if it was for only a few weeks.

She had married whilst in her early twenties to a man who ticked all the boxes that she had subconsciously created: steady, solvent, reasonably good-looking and attentive. They had both followed their respective careers, supporting one another and sharing parenting duties when their children were born, creating a comfortable life for themselves. Their children had grown up, bringing their problems to Margot's door, where they were eased by the strength of the family's bond. University, work and partners arrived in what seemed like the blink of an eye, and one day Margot woke and realized that her offspring were no longer with her. Throughout all of these years her husband had never shown any inclination of being anything other than contented with the life that he and Margot shared together, so, when she read the letter that her husband had left her on the day that he never came home, it felt like the foundations on which she had built her life had been destroyed.

Eventually he had contacted her and so began the long and protracted divorce that had only recently been settled.

It was no surprise, then, that Margot had no wish to tear the plaster off a wound that was still so raw: for her, at this moment in time, walking across silent sands in the late evening or, as was the case today, sitting and gazing at the distant mountains was enough to help to rebuild herself.

Room Three

It had been twelve months to the day when Chanai returned to the Guest House. This had been the place where her wildest hopes, dreams and desires had finally come together; the place that she held closest to her heart and the place where she always considered that her life had truly begun. This was the place that, twelve months earlier, she had chosen to retreat to from her hectic city life; a quiet seaside town where she could hide, if only for a fortnight, from everyone and everything that she knew. She had selected the guest house partly because of its location - having been born and raised in a large city, many miles from the coast, she had always had a passion for the sea - but mostly because it was a small and seemingly intimate house. When Chanai had first arrived, she had been greeted warmly by her landlady, Mrs. Mason, a woman of indeterminate age, who glowed like a ripe peach on a summer's day, and she knew that she had made the right choice of accommodation.

Chanai had begun her holiday with no expectations other than to absent herself from the pressures dictated by her job. In the city she worked creating advertising campaigns as part of a small team within a large corporate company. Her days were bookended by deadlines, demands and overly-critical clients, and, as rewarding as her work was, and as highly regarded as she was within the company, each one left her drained and tired. Publicly she was someone who could fulfil the wishes of anyone, no matter how obscure or obtuse those wishes were, but privately all she wanted to do was to let the world know who she really was: all she really wanted to do was to paint. Somewhere, between the time of her younger days and her rise in the world of advertising, Chanai felt that a part of herself had been lost; the part of her which, she felt, defined her most - her personal creativity. And so, as she had settled into her room on that very first night, twelve months ago, she began to dream of her life through different eyes.

It had come as a complete surprise to Chanai when, four days into her holiday, she met Michael, and, inexplicably to her, felt her world turn upside down. She had not been looking for love or indeed a relationship of any kind, and yet, within moments of meeting him, Chanai knew that her life would never be the same again. What grew between them over the following days was to hold them together as if they had been conjoined at birth, and, when Chanai's holiday finally came to a close, was to take Michael back to the city with her.

Chanai never really knew what exactly it was that she gave to Michael, but to her he brought the confidence to live her life as she had always dreamed. She quit her job and, whilst Michael worked, devoted her days to creating her art. She used the money that she had saved to open her own gallery in which she exhibited and sold both her own work and that of other local artists whom she admired. Chanai felt a fullness in her life that she had never experienced before: at times she wished that her whole life had been lived with this feeling, but knew that, without Michael, she would never have arrived at the place she now found herself.

And now, twelve months later, Chanai was once again sitting alone on the same bed in the same room of the same guest house. Michael was no longer around to talk with her, something she often said to the small wooden box that went everywhere with her, and now sat beside her on the bedside table, yet she knew that he would always be with her.

Room Four

Laying on his bed, Jacob Wilson scanned the latest news feeds on his mobile phone. Quickly and with great dexterity his fingers scrolled between screens. To anyone watching it would have seemed as if he were searching for something.

After several minutes of not seeing whatever it was that he was looking for Jacob decided to try a different approach. His fingers moved automatically, opened the range of social media apps that he had downloaded on his phone. Almost instantly he pulled up pages filled with comments and posts - some sharing concerns, others spouting fake information, yet more spitting vitriolic remarks his way - and he allowed a wry smile to cross his lips: "Still here, then," he muttered to himself.

The guest who had checked in and taken room four was not Jacob Wilson: or rather, Jacob Wilson was not Jacob Wilson. The name that had been signed in the reception desk register was the first one that the man who had arrived at the sleepy seaside town a little under a fortnight earlier had thought of: Jacob, because it was not dissimilar to his actual name - Jake - and Wilson because it had simply occurred to him as he put pen to paper. Deception, these days, seemed to come all too easily, Jake thought as he first printed out and then signed his fictitious name: after all, even his true name, Jake Truro, had been the invention of someone else; a third party who felt it a more suitable moniker for selling him to the public. Now it seemed to him that the name 'Jake', the one thing that connected him to his childhood, was the only genuine part of him left, the only part that had not been usurped by someone else and used to satisfy their needs. At times Jake could barely even remember his own birth name - even those who ought to have been closest to the person that he really was, and the person whom he wanted to be again, referred to him by his given stage name; Jake Truro. Now, here in this small and unnoticeable house, tucked away neatly in a remote and rarely troubled coastal town, he had begun to feel like himself once more.

Jake had always wanted to be a musician for as long as he could remember. He parents were always delighted to recount stories of him bashing a drum before he could walk and hammering out tunes on the family piano as soon as he was tall enough to reach its keys. He had sung before he could talk (parental exaggerations never seemed to cease to charm) and was never happier than when music was blaring through the house. It had begun with family friends, then moved on to anyone who they met that would listen before eventually (and hadn't all their Christmases come at once) culminating with the press. Their devotion to their son was laudable, and the light that they basked in un-dimmable.

Jake had moved from school boy bands to a band which played gigs in local pubs and clubs. Their notoriety and following began to grow - the less seriously minded or ambitious members gave way to more driven and skillful players, but Jake remained a constant. His songs (and the group's output was predominantly his work) touched a nerve with their audience, and their reputation, both by word of mouth and full-on use of social media, blossomed.

They self-released their debut album, and no one who knew them or had witnessed them perform was surprised at how well it was received. The local music press soon picked up on this, and, clearly wanting to be linked with a group who were 'going places', it wasn't long before the record companies came knocking. The band eventually signed contracts with a large record label which 'loved the freshness and direction of their music' and wanted to 'help them to reach the audience that they so richly deserved'.

A second album soon followed, its music and lyrical content very much in the same vein as the band's debut, with Jake taking the central role. Admittedly its production values were a little higher, and it certainly cost more to complete, but the band was pleased and the company, after seeing its sales figures, delighted. By the time that the third album was released the group had toured relentlessly and raked up sales that had made them each very wealthy young men. Despite this newfound luxury, however, Jake continued to produce emotionally charged and hard-hitting lyrics, tinging them with his acerbic wit, and the new material that they performed delighted the crowds.

After spending a month locked away in the recording studio, Jake and the band were pleased with the results of their labors: the album sounded strong, the songs were good and the production back to a standard that they appreciated. The record company seemed happy and ordered their charges to take 'a well-earned break - a nice holiday, somewhere hot', which they duly did.

When Jake returned, however, and met up with the record company again, he could barely believe what he heard: the album had been remixed almost to the point of being unrecognizable as having been written by the band. Harmonies had been added (where had they come from?), original vocals mixed down, guitar parts mixed up, bizarre beats laid down and melodies 'enhanced'. Initially Jake sat in the company office with an incredulous look on his face, but, before very long, the explosion came.

After much argument - and the odd (unusual and played up) tantrum - the record company backed down and agreed to put out the original version.

Of course, they released the remixed album.

Which explained why Jake, under an assumed name, was now laying on a bed in a quiet guest house, with not a living soul knowing his whereabouts.

Room Five

He had lived in the guest house for as long as he could remember, and for a few years before that - days from which he recalled nothing at all. He had grown up to know every inch of the large attic room in which he lived as if it were a close friend. During the long months of winter, when holiday makers kept to the warmth of the cities, and the flow of guests became nothing more than a trickle, he had been allowed to explore each room of the house. Systematically he had worked his way through each one, at first as a child at play, inventing games and scenarios in which he took the starring role, but later as an investigator, his notebook always in his hand. He had noted down the irregularities and foibles of each room, interrogating both the detailed notes and the rooms themselves to relieve them of their secrets and mysteries. Only when he was satisfied that each room was not hiding something from him would he move on to the next. And then, just when he felt that the previous room had relaxed and let its guard slip, he would pounce upon it, catch it unawares, and prize its darkest skeletons from its cupboards.

The notebook had grown over the years, random loose sheets and newspaper cuttings folded and tucked carefully between its pages. Its somewhat creased and battered cover of thin card had, initially, been covered in old wallpaper, taped neatly on the inside, but, as the years had worn on, it had found itself tucked inside a leather manuscript folder, held fast by thick elastic bands. From time to time new discoveries about the house had been found, and new histories revealed. Occasionally a guest or two would arrive and let slip something of themselves that might be of interest or even notoriety: names and facts found themselves duly noted and, in rare cases, newspaper cuttings discovered and added. Sometimes, though this was a rare occurrence, the notebook seemed to have taken its own interest in the characters held within its pages, following every recorded moment of their lives. Now, as George thumbed through it, he cast his mind back to his earliest memories.

He had never truly known his mother - he had been only three years old when she had died, herself still a teenager. His first true recollection of growing up had been the sound of his grandmother's voice, forceful, harsh and proud: this was a woman not to be ignored or disobeyed. He remembered, too, the playful voice of his aunt, who, although at the time seemed much older than he was, felt more like a sister to him. He thought of how, when he could begin to comprehend age, the six years between them felt like nothing and yet everything: how could he be the son of a girl not much older than the one with whom he spent his weekends playing such simple, childish games?

George's grandmother had died whilst he had been at school. He remembered the head teacher coming into the classroom - it had been a physics lesson, George recalled, and, since that day, all interest in the subject had eluded him - walking up to the teacher and whispering something to him, his back turned to the class. He had taken George from the classroom and to his austere office to break the news. His aunt, Claudette, had already been there and she had hugged him, but not in the way that she had done when they were younger in playful, short grasps or wrestling holds. Not this time. This time her hold was that of a mother clinging dearly to a child, hoping to protect them from the ills and evils of the world, yet knowing, deep down inside, that they were wishing for the impossible. Claudette hugged him and then took him back to the guest house and fed him sandwiches and cake. She performed each task as if it were automatic, as if she had known that this day would come and had prepared her actions accordingly. George, too, went through the motions, following Claudette's lead, but he too understood that, once more, his life had changed: he had been left in the care of his aunt and with his notebook as his only companion.

Claudette

When she had been four years old, Claudette's parents had decided to leave their lives in the city and move to the coast. Her father quit his job, they sold their modest house and, using the savings that they had, along with a small inheritance, bought a guest house in a quiet seaside town. They had made a conscious decision to avoid any one of the many busy coastal resorts figuring that a more modest income would be offset by having more time to spend together as a family.

Claudette was the younger of the family's two children by six years, and she had always held her sister up as an icon for her own life, so, as her sister settled comfortably into life in a small, isolated town, so did Claudette. Together they explored the beaches and dunes that rose up from the sea like golden promises. They spent endless hours digging sand and building princesses castles mounted with flags to attract imaginary princes. They built winter dens from driftwood and shells and dipped their toes in the cold, fresh sea, racing cheerfully from it as it chilled their bones. Sandwiches and bottles of fizzy pop were an everyday banquet to them and for a while life, for Claudette, was could not have been more perfect.

Things changed for Claudette during the summer that her sister turned fourteen. Her sister no longer wanted to spend her days beach-combing or pretending to be princess awaiting rescue or a dragon slaying heroine freeing her little sister. She had discovered fashion, music and magazines; her hair now sported a cut alien to the long, flowing tresses that Claudette recognized, and she seemed to spend her time watching, although for what, Claudette had no idea.

Gradually she began to spend more and more time away from the family life of which Claudette had become the focus. Sometimes Claudette didn't mind as she re-imagined the games that she and her sister had used to play, but, when the house danced to the tune of its guests, and her parents had no time for her, she felt lonely, bewildered and lost.

Claudette, of course, had no comprehension of what was going on - for her such things were a distant speck on a faraway horizon - but she remembered vividly the rage of her father and the tears of her mother as winter passed slowly into spring. She remembered too the air of silence that descended on the house and the voices that fell to a whisper when she was near. At night when sleep would not come she would sometimes hear gentle sobs coming from her parent's bedroom followed by the curses of her father.

As spring grew so did Claudette's sister, the swelling in her belly now no longer disguisable. The silence in the house gradually began to ease, but, even at her tender age, Claudette realized that nothing would be the same again.

That summer a baby boy burst into the world, full of innocence and hope, and blissfully unaware of the circumstances behind his birth. Within a year he had lost his grandfather, leaving Claudette's mother to hold the reins. As strong a woman as she was it was obvious that she missed the space once occupied by her husband - as obvious as it was that the hole that he had left would never be filled. To those closest to her it was also clear that, despite her best efforts to hide it, a resentment had built between her and her eldest daughter. Fueled by blame and guilt the rift between them simply grew wider and wider, and Claudette began to see less and less of her sister as she spent as little time as she had to with the family: George might as well have been a brother to Claudette rather than a nephew.

Claudette's sister died when she was just eighteen years of age, found on the floor of an old weather-worn and lonely beach hut, surrounded by empty bottles, cans and filthy blankets. By the time the police had arrived a pair of opportunistic crabs had already discovered her soft flesh.

Her funeral was the last time that Claudette ever saw her mother cry.

The Dream

Duncan woke to the sound of his heartbeat. Its slow, steady pounding tried to lull him back to sleep, but there was a stronger, more insistent voice that forced his eyelids open. He was alone; alone in the room in which he had awoken to the same dream since he had arrived here. The same dream which had led him to this small and overlooked coastal retreat. His skin prickled with a cold, sticky chill but he pulled back the bedsheets and made his way into the compact en-suite shower room. The water was warm and felt comforting against his body as it fell from the shower. He dried himself and walked back into the main part of his room, half expecting to find himself back in his dream. His relief at being alone allowed a grin to form across his face. He dressed himself and, having checked the time to make sure that he wasn't too early for breakfast, made his way downstairs and into the dining room.

Claudette was already there, making sure that everything was ready for her guests: bowls and plates, spoons and forks and a variety of cereals and jams were placed neatly on one large table ready for selection. She greeted Duncan jovially mentioning that he looked refreshed and well today. She asked him if he would prefer something cooked for his breakfast rather than his usual cereal and coffee. He thanked her but declined, pouring himself a small bowl of cornflakes onto which he drizzled some cold milk. He sat at a table which looked out over the street and watched the occasional passer-by as he ate, marveling at how peacefully quiet he felt. When he had eaten he returned his bowl to the table and poured himself a large mug of coffee. It surprised him a little that none of the other guests had yet come downstairs for their breakfast - Claudette had strict rules that it would be available between seven-thirty and nine-thirty, no earlier and certainly no later - but she herself now seemed to have disappeared, probably on some urgent mission to collect supplies, Duncan thought.

As he drank his coffee, Duncan wandered aimlessly around the room, studying the photographs which hung on the walls. Although this room served as both a dining room and a communal area it was still part of the house which belonged to Claudette, and it was no surprise to Duncan that, although many of the pictures featured local scenes and landmarks, there were some of a more personal nature.

There was one picture in particular that caught Duncan's attention. It was a photograph that he could not remember having seen before: perhaps it was a recent addition to the display, but perhaps also it was one that he had simply never really looked at before. It was a family group shot, taken on the beach, close to where the cliffs began to rise away from the shore. The group consisted of two adults and two children, whom he assumed were their children. The man in the photograph Duncan did not recognize, but the woman, the mother, bore a striking resemblance to Claudette - clearly this then was a family portrait. The elder of the two children, both of whom were girls, must have been, Duncan guessed, around fourteen years of age and, whilst not dissimilar from her mother in looks, carried more of her father's genes. This must, he concluded, have been Claudette's sister. There was probably about five or so years between the girls and, whilst Duncan was certain that he had never seen the older girl before, there was something about her that was strangely familiar.

— — —

Margot found herself behind the wheel of her car. She was parked up by the side of the road, the small town that she had last driven through now far behind her, when the tears came. With no destination she had been driving for what seemed like hours, although now, for her, time itself had lost all meaning or relevance. She had climbed into the car in the hope that it would provide protection, or at least a distraction, and take her far from the steadily cracking ground upon which she had been standing. She had driven through the suburbs, hard and fast, intent only on escape; escape from the city and escape from the rapidly unravelling memories upon which she now felt her life had been built. The streets and houses had all fled by without notice, hiding their faces in the shadows as the car sped past them. Its tires hissed angrily on the still-wet tarmac as if they were somehow complicit in her rage. As she reached the quieter streets the lights began to grow dimmer, less frequent, as if even they were feeling the same pain that Margot was. The anger inside her now was beginning to evolve into something else, something far more complex and destructive. She felt a wave of disappointment suddenly hit her and, as she gasped for air, it seemed as if it would drag her beneath itself and drown her. With it it brought an overwhelming sensation of loss, as if twenty-seven years of marriage had simply vanished, leaving no trace of her life or who she was. And then there was the shock, the sense of injustice that, after all that he had said to her, and all that she had said to him - the promises and little intimacies that stretched between couples like spider silk - the words ultimately meant nothing: in the end the attraction of youth held sway over everything. And youth it was, it seemed to Margot, which had wrenched her husband from her and led him to the arms and then the bed of another. She had no idea, no indication, of who this other woman was - her husband had not even afforded her that dignity - but she wondered if this woman, this home-breaker, might not have been merely a younger version of herself.

Through the darkened streets the car raced on, Margot, behind the steering wheel, thinking nothing of where she was going, but everything about where she was headed. How could she live a life without everything that she had once held as true? Would she want to try to begin her life over again? Was it even possible? At forty-nine she thought it almost inconceivable that she would find herself in a situation in which there was nothing upon which she could rely; a situation that would involve her building a new life from the ashes of the old. She had always thought that, by the time she had reached this age, her life would be settled and assured; that time now would allow herself the luxury of living for herself and not simply living to survive - that her struggles might finally be over.

Without warning the car shuddered, lurching violently towards the middle of the road. Instinctively Margot tightened her grip on the steering wheel, pulling the car back towards the curb. The car skidded, and she quickly turned the wheel in the opposite direction. For a moment the vehicle zig-zagged along the road, its speed barely diminished, and Margot felt like she might lose control of it but, almost as if the car could read her thoughts, it righted itself, finding its path once more.

Margot felt her muscles relax involuntarily and she exhaled deeply as if releasing everything that had been preoccupying her. Her focus was, for the first time, now solely on the road ahead. She wondered if, perhaps, she had had a blow-out in one of the tires, but realized that, as the car was driving normally now, that this could not have been the case. Perhaps she had hit something, a fox, perhaps. She glanced automatically in her rear-view mirror, but by now she was too far from the incident to have seen anything, even if it had not been so late at night. Briefly she thought about turning the car around and heading back, but, if she had hit an animal at the speed that she had been travelling at, there would have been nothing that she could have done for it. The analogy of the potential fate of the animal and what had happened to her smashed into her brain like a slab of concrete. She braked hard, sliding the car into the grass verge at the edge of the road.

In the guest house Margot woke bathed in sweat.

— — —

Duncan left the house but found himself surrounded by darkness. Despite the fact that it was still early morning - and, as he had eaten his breakfast, drunk his coffee and looked out over the street, the daylight had reflected the usual passing by of those with places to go - once outside Duncan appeared to have slipped backwards (or forwards) into the middle of the night. Instinctively he turned around, as if by checking the house he would be able to understand what had happened, and somehow find himself back in daylight. The house looked different to him and, although he could neither explain what he was seeing or register how it was happening, the house appeared to gradually fade and morph itself into a different, more modern residence. Quickly Duncan turned back to check the street; it too was no longer the same. The road stretched out away from him in both directions for as far as he could see in the darkness. Opposite him the houses were set back from the road behind gardens some of which were open to the grey pavement in front of them whilst others snuggled safely behind hedges and fences. When he looked to his right he could see them begin to thin and gradually fade from view as the street lights gave way to blackness. Everything was calm, still and silent. Looking away to the left, Duncan could see a fan of light rising up from what was clearly a city or town: a stark contrast to the scene now in front of him. Before he had a chance to begin to wonder how he had left one place and arrived in another he heard the sound of footsteps on the far side of the street and away to his left. Out of the gloom Duncan could just make out the figure of a man, dressed in dark clothing, running. He was heading out of the town (or suburb of the city, Duncan couldn't say for certain exactly which was the case) and out towards the countryside. His pace seemed regular and steady and Duncan guessed that he was a late-night jogger, patrolling his usual run. As he drew nearer to Duncan, albeit on the opposite side of the road, Duncan's attention was caught by a second sound, once more coming from a place away to his left: the sound of an engine. The noise was harsh, cutting, as it did, through the silence of the night with little regard for either the sleeping or the nocturnal.

The car came into view. Duncan watched as the man moved, without breaking his stride, into the road. He could hear the music over the sound of the engine now, over the sound of bone crunching against metal and tarmac and over the cries of shock and pain. Duncan watched as the car began to weave along the road, shuddering and lurching from side to side before he lost sight of it in the darkness. He knew that moments like this were supposed to happen in slow motion, but it hadn't; events had happened before Duncan even had time to register what he was seeing. Far too late to block things out, he closed his eyes.

— — —

He was floating now, hovering over Chanai's body like a ghost, but she knew he was far more than that. Unable to move her arms she willed him to lower his body, to reach down and touch her. Needing no more encouragement than her thoughts, Michael followed her every wish. At last she could feel the weight of him upon her once more, lighter than she remembered but then he had always been a considerate lover. She felt his arms wrap around her then begin to sink beneath her skin as if trying to hold her soul, the essence of who she was. The sheets slipped from the bed and her pajamas from her body. She was naked now and she noticed that he was too. His skin felt cool against her and she could sense the heat flow from her body to his making them one - the one that she knew that they were.

In her dream they made love in silence. There was no need for words to pass between them - each knew the most private intimacies of the other, the touches that would free them and those that would bind. For Chanai there could be nothing more, nothing less: she had found her heaven, her Nirvana, and she knew that nothing could take this feeling from her.

Afterwards, as they lay next to each other, Chanai noticed how much paler now Michael's flesh was against her dark skin. She squeezed his hand tightly, as if to reassure him that it didn't matter, but she already knew that he would only grow paler with time. She stared up at the ceiling and listened to their breathing until she could no longer distinguish between their breaths, and as she did he began to hum softly. For a while she lay still, listening to the melody flow from him, worried that any movement from her might break the spell and end the dream. Gradually, however, the pull of the song, and all that it meant, became too great for her to resist and she began to quietly sing the lyric, mouthing each word before releasing it to the air above her:

But if I'd never caught your eye,
And if I'd never seen your smile,
Would I be still left wondering why?
And would it have been worth the while?

Chanai allowed her eyes to close as she repeated the refrain over and over again knowing that soon all of this would fall away from her and that reality would return. But, for now, all she wanted was to hold on to the dream for a little while longer.

— — —

When Duncan opened his eyes, he was standing once more outside the front door of the guest house. He was unsure of what had just happened, and what he had just seen - if, indeed, he had actually seen anything. Perhaps, he thought, he had been daydreaming, or maybe even had had a flashback to some memory that he had buried long ago. Perhaps he was still dreaming. But no. He was certain that he had woken, gone downstairs and eaten breakfast; he had even spoken to his landlady, Mrs. Mason. His hand reached out and gripped the handle of the door: it felt solid and real beneath his grasp. He turned it and stepped back inside the house.

The doorway was dark, and it took a moment for Duncan's eyes to adjust to the sudden lack of light. As shapes made themselves visible to him he realized that he was standing not in the hallway of the guest house but on the threshold of a room whose layout was not dissimilar to his own. Day had once more given way to night, but what was more disconcerting to Duncan, however, was the fact that this, despite its similarities, was not his room, and he felt a wave of unease as he looked across at the figure laying asleep on the bed. In the darkness he could make out the contours of her young body beneath the sheet, her chest rising and falling steadily, her face glowing slightly in the hint of moonlight which crept between the curtains. He wondered how, if she were to suddenly awake, he would be able to explain his presence, yet he also felt unable to move, as if he had become a figure in a painting.

The woman, he had by now realized, was, like him, also one of the guests in the house - he had seen her in the mornings and exchanged pleasantries with her most days - but beyond that he knew nothing of her. As he stood, transfixed, he became aware of a shadow, lighter in hue than the surrounding night, but clearly visible, forming itself close to his shoulder.

Gradually it began to take the form of a gaseous cloud, roughly the size and shape of a man, but grey and featureless. It floated slowly towards the woman's bed, hovering over it for a few moments before lowering and spreading itself until it had consumed her body. By now the bed itself had begun to become part of the cloud of grey and it was impossible to ascertain where it was in relation to the rest of the room. For a moment Duncan felt that he was part of the gaseous cloud: his arms and legs seemed to lose contact with anything solid and his body seemed weightless, floating towards the bed. A cold moistness filtered through his skin and crept along his bones like an army of ants heightening his awareness of everything around him. He could see the young woman clearly now, her recumbent figure rocking gently, but, more than this, he somehow found himself able to feel what she was feeling and to experience what she was experiencing.

And then the cloud was gone, and he was standing once more in the darkened doorway, his ears filled with the words that she was singing in her sleep; words that were somehow strangely familiar to him:

But if I'd never caught your eye,
And if I'd never seen your smile,
Would I be still left wondering why?
And would it have been worth the while?

— — —

The water was closing in now, swirling overhead like thunder clouds marching across the sky, steadily swallowing the blue. Shapes that had once been distinguishable shivered and shook in the glinting light before becoming merely colors floating above the water. The bright blue tried to reach out one last time, an arm, glistening in the dying light, plunging into the waves. And then blackness.

Jake felt himself sinking; down and down and down he went, his clutching hands and fingers useless, finally giving up their attempts to grab at anything that might save him. On his back, and looking up at the rapidly receding surface, Jake was aware that he was not dead: he had sunk until the land above him had disintegrated into little more than a memory, and yet he had not drowned. He could feel his chest steadily rising and falling against the pressure of the water as it sought to crush him, and he realized that he was breathing, as if he were cocooned in a bubble. Strange creatures floated first towards and then past his still sinking form. In the darkness he struggled to try to make out their form; to recognize and put a name to them. Gradually his eyes became used to the dimness that surrounded him, and his body to the cold that it was feeling. He tried to reach out, to touch the aquatic creatures as they passed him, but, as he did, they seemed to melt from his grasp as if they weren't really there - as if their shape and form existed only in his imagination. And then he realized that these shapes, these bizarre and imaginary creatures which were swimming around him, were not animal in nature, but words. Floating beneath the gently undulating current, Jake watched as the words began to form themselves into random phrases and lines, some meaningless, some emotive and others bordering on the profound. Without giving his situation a second thought, he breathed in deeply sucking the words towards himself. He watched as they danced in front of his eyes, rearranging themselves, refining their meaning, before they snaked their way up his nostrils and disappeared. Deep inside his mind he could feel them jostling, forming and reforming themselves into verses, choruses and refrains. None seemed familiar to him and he hoped desperately that, if he were ever to find himself back on land again, he would be able to recall them.

Through the grey water, the words continued to come, wave upon wave, until Jake felt that he was drowning for a second time. A small collection gathered itself in front of his eyes, close, but tantalizingly out of his reach. They neither swept passed him or allowed themselves to be absorbed into his body, and he could do nothing but watch as they grouped themselves into an order which he recognized instantly. The words hung in the water as if they were dangling on the end of a rope or noose. As they did so, more words appeared, arranging themselves beneath the first line until they had formed a stanza that Jake knew only too well; a stanza that even the most skilled group of monkeys, given all the time and technology in the world, would have struggled to hit upon - a stanza that had formed itself first in Jake's brain so many months earlier. His whole body seemed now to shudder and sway gently as he felt the melody ease from his pores, filling the ocean around him. Without his lips even parting he could hear the words swim free from himself:

But if I'd never caught your eye,
And if I'd never seen your smile,
Would I be still left wondering why?
And would it have been worth the while?

— — —

When Duncan turned around and stepped out of the room he found himself on a jetty. He checked behind himself and saw that the jetty was long and jutted out almost precariously over the ocean, its wooden planks weather-worn and tired. With one footstep Duncan had found himself almost at the head of the pier, although, by now, he had given up trying to fix logic and reasoning to the day's events. It was early morning once more: a warm sun had already burned the clouds from the sky and a prickly heat had begun to creep over the land beneath the sky. Duncan could feel the warmth on the back of his neck and his naked forearms and wondered if this was some kind of sign that his day would indeed begin to make sense.

The grey sea stretched out away from him, its slate surface broken only fleetingly by the current which was dragging it unerringly towards the shore. Leaning forwards, his arms resting on the wooden rail which ran along the top of the fencing which ran alongside most of the jetty, Duncan stared into the water. At first, he saw nothing but the water looking back at him as if it recognized him as a long lost, half-forgotten friend, but, as his eyes began to adjust themselves to the disruptive properties of the water, he started to make out details in the shapes that he could see. The seaweed swayed and parted, its heavy fronds abandoning their weight to the up thrust; fish skittered across his line of vision, darting and diving, and surfacing occasionally to gulp at the warm air; once in a while a gull would appear and dive beneath the surface, but the fish were awake to the danger, and the gulls returned to flight disappointed.

As he continued to stare into the water, his gaze going ever deeper, Duncan became aware of a new shape which seemed to be forming itself in ever more detail. It was a shape that he would never have associated with the sea, and certainly not one that he would have expected to have seen. Below the surface of the water the shape began to reveal its features in ever greater detail. There was no mistaking the identity of the shape that Duncan was seeing now: it was clear. It was the body of a man.

Not for the first time, Duncan found himself paralyzed, unable to move or act, even if he had wanted to or known what to do. He felt as if he were an audience of one, watching a film play out before his eyes, and, at the very moment when the endangered character on the screen was pleading for help, he was unable to give it: he had been drawn in and made part of the action, given the role of potential hero, and then been chained to a rock, inert and ineffectual, destined to merely watch as the world about him crumbled.

Below him the body seemed to float as if suspended somewhere between the surface of the water and the ocean bed. Despite the greyness of the water and the brightness of the sunlight Duncan was seeing it in ever greater detail: black denim jeans, soaked now in the brine, clung tightly to the man's legs, his feet held firm in expensive looking boots. He was wearing a t-shirt, also black, which bore a picture of a group that Duncan enjoyed listening to, but this was looser and danced across his torso with the underwater currents. His eyes were wide open and staring as if they were fixed upon something in the water that Duncan could not see and, as bubbles of air began to rise from him lips towards the water's surface, Duncan realized that he knew the man, or at least he recognized him: it was another of the residents in the guest house - Jacob.

At the exact moment in which this realization hit Duncan he became aware of music filling the air around him. He was unsure of exactly where it was coming, but he could have sworn that it was rising from the sea; or more specifically from the body beneath it. The tune swam for moment inside Duncan's head awakening recollections of where he had heard it before. As it replayed in his mind he became aware of the words that he had heard Chanai singing in her sleep just moments earlier, first hovering over it and then seamlessly joining with it and becoming one. He realized, too, where he had heard the song before: stood, by the side of a quiet road, watching as a car plowed through the figure of a running man.

– – –

Often, as George slept, his dreams would be filled with the stories from the pages of his notebooks: some happy, some sad; some full of hope and promise, others tinged with tragedy and despair. Each had begun as a seed, built upon a comment that he had overheard or an action he had witnessed which had made it between the pages of his journal, where it was nurtured and tended until it had grown and taken on its own life. So many of the guests had found their way onto George's pages that by now some of their stories have become entwined, curling themselves around one another like climbing plants until one had become indistinguishable from the other, but some had remained strong and independent, able to fight off the intentions of their weaker, more parasitic neighbors: there were the two couples who had arrived separately, strangers to each other, but had left together, each partner in the arms of the other; the once famous comedian whose television career had hit the rocks and who now scratched out a living as a warm-up act in small seaside theatres; there was the con-man, who had worked the local seaside towns for several years who was finally caught, red-handed by the police in the living room; and the elderly couple who smiled at one another but whispered in corners of the end and were discovered one morning, their bodies still clinging tightly to one another. There was the former star of the movies who had turned her back on fame and its trappings and taken to travelling and holidaying in obscure and sleepy towns; and the man who came and stayed for a week who questioned Claudette whenever he could and looked at George in a strange way.

Of course George only had his imagination and his notebooks to guide him in his fantasies - he had no other way of knowing whether or not the stories that he had composed in his head bore out in reality (apart from incidents such as the make or break holiday which ended in a suicide - although even then George's timeline of events had taken on its own life) - but, to him, every element of every story held its own truth.

This particular night, however, George's mind, so accustomed to following the flow of his dreams, was disturbed and unable to focus. As usual he had gone to his bed at ten o'clock and spent around half an hour adding to his journal, reading through the previous handful of entries to see how the days hung together. He had begun to focus on one single event, certain that this would set his dreams off, as this process generally did, along the path that he had chosen. Tonight, however, his rest came fitfully, images tumbling in and out of his mind seemingly at random, leading him first one way and then another as he fought for control. He saw a faceless figure - a man - his arms wrapped about a girl. Her face resembled his aunt in the photographs that he had seen of her in her youth. The man stepped slowly back from her and began to fade and disappear, his arms stretched out as if he was unwilling to let her go.

He saw a middle-aged couple in the throes of an argument, truths and accusations being flung like spears; he saw a younger couple embracing, making love as if time were endless; he saw a man pursued by robotic, suited figures, his clothes dissolving into a jumble of words; he saw a speeding car and a tear-soaked face; a body, cold and laid out like meat at a buffet; he saw the water and could taste the lies. And always, in each scene, he saw the same figure; the same faceless man, standing, watching with sightless eyes like a dying vulture. And always he heard the same refrain, repeating itself over and over again, falling like a backdrop as the scenes were replayed:

But if I'd never caught your eye,
And if I'd never seen your smile,
Would I be still left wondering why?
And would it have been worth the while?

― ― ―

Duncan woke to the sound of his heartbeat. Its slow, steady pounding tried to lull him back to sleep, but there was a stronger, more insistent voice that forced his eyelids open. Slowly, as if fearful that any sudden movement might break the moment, he raised his head from between the woman's thighs. He looked up, for the first time, gazing over her slender torso and young, tender breasts. Gradually her face began to come into his line of sight, its smooth contours and flushed skin making themselves known to him slowly, inch by inch. When his eyes met hers, he knew her instantly as the girl he had seen in the photograph - the girl who had stood so close to Claudette.

As he looked at her, at the face that, for so many nights now, he had longed to see, he felt horrified as he watched her begin to change. Slowly she began to lose the rosy glow that she had worn only moments before. The color started to seep gradually from her face until she became pallid and white, her skin drained of blood, as if she had become a mannequin. Her eyes, so bright and full of passion just seconds earlier, now resembled marbles, their glassy stare inhuman and cold. She was completely still by now and, as he touched her smooth flesh, Duncan felt an icy shiver pass from her and into him.

— — —

George sat on his bed, awake now and surrounded by his notebooks, each one them open, the words tumbling from them like autumn leaves in a storm. He could feel the characters whose lives he had chronicled taking shape around him, filling the room like ghosts, gradually sucking the air from the room. Behind his eyes his memories lined up, each one ready to attach itself to the person to whom it belonged, as George's visions slowly circled him. Inside himself, George fought to hold on to each one, but his grip was weaker than he had hoped and, one by one, they tore themselves from him. With each lost memory George felt a part of him vanish into the spaces in the room as if he were nothing more than a collection of stories and, as each one disappeared so he became less and less of who he thought that he was.

He shivered as he felt the walls of the house begin to shudder and the timbers creak and moan under the weight of dead pasts. Stories tumbled out of George like moths bursting from cocoons, crashing haphazardly into the window, trying to live before their light faded and their wings disintegrated like leaves in winter. And now the walls themselves began to crack and crumble around him, dust seeping from them like all the tears he had never cried: tears for those who had come and then gone; tears for those for whom the guest house had proven not to be the answer; tears for Claudette, his grandmother, his mother and tears for himself. He watched as, brick by brick, the house began to vanish around him, leaving nothing but his bed and his fast emptying books. George lay back, closed his eyes and silently prayed for the dream to return.

Your hands tremble

and your lips quiver

while the screen's glow of static

reflects within your dry eyes

the crackle of greys and blacks and white.

Dreams become reality.

Author Biographies

Patrick Walts is the author of three books, *"Effugium: The Time Remaining"*, *"The Act of Laughting"* and *"Liberty"*. He's currently writing a sequel to *"Effugium"* entitled *"Exsilium"* and an anthology of short stories entitled *"Grave Concerns"*. He currently resides in Oklahoma City, Oklahoma with his wife and their menagerie of spoiled, bratty animals.

Blog: *patrickwaltsfiction.wordpress.com*

Amazon Author Page: *amazon.com/Patrick-Walts/e/B008ZNY36Q*

***

tara caribou is a storyteller at heart. An avid reader of hard science fiction and modern poetry, you will most often find her writing short stories and poetry barefoot on some rural Alaskan beach or out in the woods. When not writing, she's reading, sleeping, cooking, watching the local wildlife or staring out at the stars, where her heart continually wanders in the cold.

Blog: Raw Earth Ink at *taracaribou.com*

Instagram: *https://www.instagram.com/tara_caribou*

Buy: *http://www.lulu.com/spotlight/taracaribou*

***

River Dixon has unknowingly found himself trapped in the incessant heat and beauty of Arizona. It is here, along with his family, that he finds solace stringing together words in an attempt to find a structure or sequence that may one day make sense of all this.

River can be found hanging out at The Stories In Between, where he shares his poetry and short fiction.

Blog: The Stories In Between at *thestoriesinbetween.com*

Amazon Author Page: *amazon.com/author/riverdixon*

***

Mark Towse After a 30-year hiatus, Mark recently gave up a lucrative career in sales to pursue his dream of being a writer. He has only been writing short stories for seven months now, but already his passion and belief has resulted in many prestigious magazines including *Books N' Pieces, Artpost Magazine, Flash Fiction Magazine, Horrorzine, Antipodean SF, Page & Spine, Twenty-Two Twenty-Eight and Montreal Writes.* Two of his stories have been produced on *The No Sleep Podcast* and six anthologies set for later this year will include his stories also.

Blog: *https://marktowsedarkfiction.wordpress.com/*

Twitter: *https://twitter.com/MarkTowsey12*

***

M. Ennenbach is a lot of things. Poet. Writer. Father. Fool. He writes from the heart and with emotion that may be strange, raw, or disturbing. He is from Illinois but lives in Texas. His kids are the most important part of his life. His books *Notches* and *(un)poetic* can be found at any major book seller.

Amazon Author Page: *https://www.amazon.com/M.-Ennenbach/e/B07P12Z1R3*

Blog: Mike's Manic Word Depot *at mennenbach.com*

***

Sam "Goldie" Kirk, with a master's degree in Global Business Management, is a full-time paper pusher living in the

Northern Hemisphere. Sam always seeks writing opportunities – from being a writer for school papers, through an Assistant Editor-in-Chief position of a university magazine, to now being a blogger with over 1,500 followers.

Sam is passionate about writing mystery, dark fiction, YA, and anything that involves a bit of psychology. Having lived on various continents, he likes to start discussions and explore diverse stories. Sam does his best writing on top of a mountain, by a river, or in the forest clearing.

To stay golden, connect on Twitter or via his website.

Twitter: @EnneaGramType8

Blog: https://dailyflabbergast.wordpress.com/

***

Christopher Allen Waldrop is a library assistant. He lives in Nashville, Tennessee with his wife and multiple Dalmatians, although he can occasionally be found in other places and sometimes nowhere at all. An avid collector of graffiti among other things, he's written art criticism for a local publication.

Blog: Freethinkers Anonymous at *http://freethinkersanonymous.com/*

***

Chris Nelson was born in a small town in the east of England but grew up in Birmingham. After leaving school he studied computing at what was then Wolverhampton Polytechnic, before deciding that it was not a career path he wanted to follow. He retrained as a teacher and has taught in a primary school in Dudley since the mid-1980s.

He lives in Stourbridge with his wife and two children.

Blog: *chrisnelson61.wordpress.com*

Robert "Bobby" Blade is a resident of Southern California, his career as a Draftsman has spanned over 14 years, working for several architectural firms throughout the Los Angeles area. His love of writing came early on, inspired to write stories from watching thought-provoking shows like The Twilight Zone. He is a fan of authors like Ray Bradbury, George R.R. Martin, and Stephen King. In recent years, he has taken writing seriously and hopes to develop his craft and be considered a true writer of fiction.

***

Mark Ryan was born in Oxford, growing up in the shadow of dreaming spires. He studied film at London Metropolitan University, graduating to MA in Film Theory.

He has published collections of poetry with *Echoes in Space, Graffitied Heart,* and *Drifting in and out of Sleep. Keep it Together* is his contribution to the murder mystery arena as well as his short story collection, *Impermanence of Things.*

The Gospel of No One is a poetry fiction hybrid novel, focusing on religious imagery and the inner workings and broken pieces of the soul.

His work leans, bends, and sways to the metaphysical and supernatural, with a tendency to dabble in the macabre. Questioning questions and searching for answers in the eye of the storm, where there is always hope.

Fun bio here: *markryanhavoc.com/about*

Blog: Havoc and Consequences at *https://havocandconsequence.wordpress.com/*

Website: *https://www.markryanhavoc.com/*

Amazon: *https://www.amazon.co.uk/MARK-RYAN/e/B00PUHJLBM*